Puffin Books

☆ TH
OF AM

The Puffin Book of A ... e
to this exciting and ...se
terms, Simon Kelner unravels the intricacies of how the
game is played, captures the glamour of the National Football League competition in America which climaxes in the
Super Bowl, and describes the tumultuous evolution of the
sport with its many great and extraordinary figures.

Also learn about the skills and training required by
players, the growth of teams and competitions in Britain and
elsewhere, and the signals used by the officials. Particularly
interesting are the profiles of each of the 28 professional
clubs in the NFL, their origins, triumphs and outstanding
personalities.

Find out for yourself why the Super Bowl commands
some of the largest audiences in television history in its
homeland, and why its popularity in Britain has grown at
such an astounding rate since it first burst on to British
television screens in 1982. If you aren't a fan already, you
will be once you've read this absorbing book; if you have
already been bitten by the American football bug, it will
prove an invaluable source of information.

Simon Kelner was born in Manchester and trained as a
journalist in South Wales. He was formerly assistant sports
editor of the *Observer* and is now deputy sports editor of
the *Independent*, for which he writes the weekly American
football column.

THE ★ PUFFIN ★ BOOK ★ OF
AMERICAN FOOT ★ BALL

Illustrated by Bob Harvey

PUFFIN BOOKS

Puffin Books, Penguin Books Ltd, Harmondsworth, Middlesex, England
Viking Penguin Inc., 40 West 23rd Street, New York, New York 10010, USA
Penguin Books Australia Ltd, Ringwood, Victoria, Australia
Penguin Books Canada Ltd, 2801 John Street, Markham, Ontario, Canada L3R 1B4
Penguin Books (NZ) Ltd, 182–190 Wairau Road, Auckland 10, New Zealand

First published 1987

Made and printed in Great Britain by
Cox & Wyman Ltd, Reading

Filmset in Rockwell Medium (Linotron 202) by
Rowland Phototypesetting Ltd,
Bury St Edmunds, Suffolk

To Karen, for your love

CONTENTS

INTRODUCTION

WHEN Channel 4 began their weekly American football programme in 1982, they set in motion one of the most remarkable recent trends in British sport. From nowhere sprang a large and enthusiastic following for a game that, previously, had been viewed by British eyes as a bizarre and unfathomable ritual.

Instantly, it seemed, a sizeable chunk of the nation was hooked on the glamour and excitement of American football, and before long the curiosity and instant appeal turned into a thirst to learn more about this alien sport. Today, the game is not so strange in Britain. The upsurge in interest gave rise to a desire to play the game and, currently, there are 120 organized and fully kitted-out teams in Britain playing in a national league.

The viewing figure for Channel 4's Sunday evening highlights programme is now between two and three million, and it is largely a knowledgeable audience. Yet because the game can appear complicated, and as we in Britain have no long tradition in American football, there are always facets which baffle even the most experienced watcher. Hence the purpose of this book.

By explaining in basic and simple terms how play evolves, and then going on to discuss strategies and more involved aspects, this book aims to educate those who have a sketchy knowledge of the game and want to start at the beginning, and also to fill in the gaps for those who already have some understanding of how American football works.

In short, I hope that in the following pages there is enough information and background to give an appreciation and comprehension of one of the world's most colourful and thrilling sports.

Simon Kelner
March 1987

1 HOW THE GAME IS PLAYED

WHEN the seasoned war-campaigner Marshal Foch returned to the United States after the First World War, he took one look at an American football match and said, 'My God! This game is war! It has everything.' First impressions of the sport would tend to back up this view – American football is brutal, the action frantic, and it can often seem as frighteningly confused and complicated as trench warfare.

In order to start making sense of the game, it is essential to strip away the complexity, put aside the vast array of rules and regulations and look at it on the simplest level. Then it is not quite so difficult to fathom, for there are basic similarities between American football and the game of rugby, with which the British are familiar.

Like rugby, it is a handling and passing game played with an oval-shaped ball, the prime objective being to cross the opposition goal line with the ball and the only method of stopping the opposition being to tackle the ball-carrier to the ground. The shape of the goalposts, in between which successful goal kicks must pass, is also common to both games.

These fundamental likenesses help initial understanding of the game, but, although American football originally derived from rugby, it developed on totally separate lines from the latter part of the nineteenth century, and the two sports are today no more than distant cousins.

To British eyes, therefore, there is much that is unfamiliar and baffling in American football. As a first step in unravelling its mysteries, it is wise to start with the basics. And there is nothing more basic – or important – than the item the players spend the whole game fighting for, the *ball*.

An American football is roughly the same oval shape as a rugby ball, but is slightly more pointed at the ends. Its length is between 11 and 11¼ inches and it weighs between 14 and 15 ounces. The official ball, used in all NFL matches, bears the name of its manufacturer, Wilson, and also the signature of NFL Commissioner Pete Rozelle.

THE BALL

The ball, light tan in colour, is made from leather. For every NFL game, the home team must provide twenty-four balls for use.

The playing surfaces in professional football vary from stadium to stadium, with an almost equal split between grass and artificial turf, but the *pitch* itself remains the same in terms of dimensions.

The American football pitch is rectangular and measures 120 yards long by 53 yards wide. These measurements have remained the same since the late 1800s when the game was first developed by Walter Camp at Yale (see Chapter 6). In fact, the unusual width comes from Camp's attempts to make the game more open by increasing the size of the pitch, 53 yards being the widest it could be to fit into a newly built stadium at Harvard.

As American football is primarily a game about the gaining of set amounts of territory (the team with the ball has four attempts to make 10 yards), the pitch is lined at 5-yard intervals. From its grid-like appearance comes American football's other name, gridiron football.

Additionally, there are small marks – called hashmarks – which are one yard apart so that the amount of yardage made can be assessed accurately. Every 10 yards there are numbers with an arrow pointing towards the nearer goal line, making it simple to see where play is at any time. For example, if a team has the ball on the line which bisects the figure 40 and the arrow is pointing behind them, they are said to be on their own 40-yard line. If the arrow is pointing ahead of them, they are in their opponents' half, 40 yards from their goal line.

The playing area of the pitch is 100 yards long, so each team's territory measures 50 yards, with the halfway line known as the midfield stripe. The pitch is bounded by sidelines, and if the ball goes beyond these lines it is out of bounds. At both ends of the pitch are the end zones, which are where the points are scored and which both teams seek to defend. Each team's end zone is 10 yards deep, and is entered by crossing the goal line.

Goalposts are set in the end lines. The distance between the uprights is 8ft 6in and the crossbar is 10ft above the ground. They are supported by a single strut, giving them the appearance of a tuning fork.

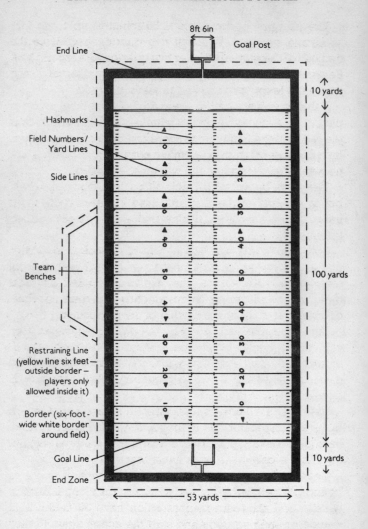

THE FIELD

How the Game is Played

The *duration* of the game is 60 minutes, split into four 15-minute quarters. The first two quarters represent the first half of the game, the latter two quarters the second half. Between the two halves, there is a 15-minute interval during which the teams are allowed to leave the field.

If the scores are tied at the end of normal time, an extra period of a maximum of 15 minutes (called overtime) is played, and the first team to score any points is the winner. In NFL play-off games, as many overtime periods as are necessary to determine the winner are played.

The game begins with a kick-off, as does the second half, but at the end of the first and third quarters there is an interval of 2 minutes and play proceeds without another kick-off.

Both teams are entitled to stop the clock and take a time-out. They can do this three times in each half, and the time-outs last 90 seconds. They are usually called at crucial times for the players to discuss tactics with their coaches, or instead to disrupt the rhythm of the opposition.

Time-outs are also called by the officials to confer with each other on penalty awards, to measure yardage gained, or to attend to an injured player. On all these occasions, the game clock, which is visible to everyone in the stadium, is stopped.

There is a further stoppage when there are 2 minutes left in the second and fourth quarters. At this point the referee halts play to warn players and coaches of the time remaining. This is called the two-minute warning.

The clock also stops running when the ball is out of bounds. When the ball is ready for play, the referee blows a whistle and the team in possession have 30 seconds to decide on their strategy and start the action again. If they take longer than 30 seconds, they are penalized.

All these stoppages – and American football is by nature a stop-start game – mean that, although actual playing time is 1 hour, a game can take as much as 3½ hours to complete.

What's more, it must be the only sport which has advertising breaks. When a game is televised, the referees stop the game so that the commercials can be broadcast.

The *teams* have forty-five players each, although only eleven are allowed on the pitch at any one time. Every man has his specialized position and in the squad there are usually two or three to cover every position. From the forty-five players, each team broadly splits up into three units: the offensive (attacking) unit to be brought on the field when they have the ball in their possession; the defensive unit, called into action when the opposition have the ball; and a special unit of players brought on for specialized plays like kick-offs, goal attempts or when the side chooses to punt (kick) the ball. The numbers the players have on their shirts may appear confusing and random but they do relate to their respective positions.

Having established the basics, we are now ready for play, which begins with the *kick-off*. Just before the game is due to start, the referee tosses a coin and the captain who guesses correctly can decide whether his side will take the kick-off or receive the ball from the kick-off. He may instead decide to play in a certain direction, in which case his opposite number has the option over the kick-off. Whoever loses the toss has the choice of what to do at the start of the second half.

To start the game, both teams send their special kick-off units on to the field, and the team which has to kick off does so from their own 35-yard line. The ball is placed on a 3-inch plastic tee and the kicker, with his ten team-mates behind him, tries to kick the ball as high and as far as possible (it must travel at least 10 yards).

His colleagues follow up the kick, which is generally gathered by a member of the opposing team – a player is designated as the kick returner – and he attempts to run with the ball back at them.

If the kick goes out of bounds, it is re-taken and, as a penalty, it is now taken from 5 yards further back (i.e. the 30-yard line). If it rolls through the opposition end zone without anyone touching it, play recommences with possession for the non-kicking team at their 20-yard line. No member of the kicking team is allowed to touch the ball unless an opponent has touched it first.

So to the first *play* of the game. Wherever the receiving team are halted, that is tackled in possession (or, if the ball ran through the end zone, on their 20-yard line), the ball is 'spotted' and play recommences from that spot. The team who have the ball (the receiving team) are now the 'offense' and the team without the ball the 'defense', and they each send their respective units on to the field. An imaginary line, where the ball is spotted, is known as the 'line of scrimmage', and both teams line up facing each other on either side of the line.

The offense must have at least seven of their eleven men on the line of scrimmage, although they can spread across the width of the pitch as they wish. The defense can put as many or as few of their players on the line providing that, in between them and the opposing team, there is a 'neutral zone' – which measures the length of a football – into which no player can go until the ball is in play. This has the effect of keeping the teams apart before the action begins.

Every time the attacking team's progress is halted – by

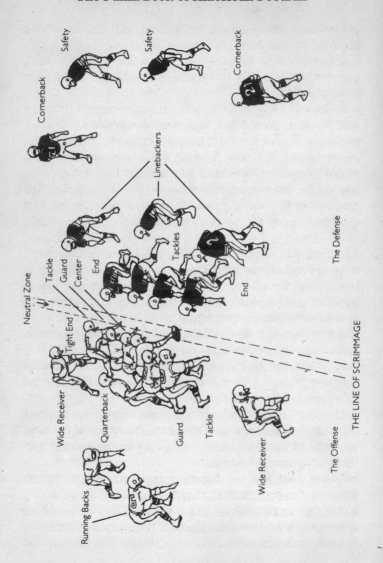

How the Game is Played

the ball-carrier being tackled (a tackle is deemed to have been made when the ball-carrier has at least one knee on the ground), or by the ball going out of bounds or being dropped to the ground – the same procedure to restart play is applied.

From this position, the attacking team must gain 10 yards, and they have four plays, or *downs*, within which to do so. When they receive the ball for the first time (from a kick-off, or when the opposition fumble the ball or punt it) they are said to have 'first down and 10', from the point where they are halted. This means that they now have the first of their four attempts to gain ground, and have 10 yards to go. If they succeed in progressing 10 yards or more within their allotted four downs, they are awarded another series of four downs to progress a further 10 yards down the field. This is how a team moves towards their opponents' goal line, and a sequence of first downs (successful attempts to gain 10 yards) allows a team to keep the ball. Their march downfield is known as a 'drive'.

As long as the offense keep gaining the required yardage, they remain in possession of the ball.

Play is restarted on each down by an action called the 'snap'. A player on the offense, the centre, stands on the line of scrimmage over the ball, which is flat on the ground, with his legs stretched wide, and on a given signal he passes the ball back through his legs to another member of his side, the *quarterback*, who is standing only inches behind him. The ball is now in motion.

The quarterback is the most important player in any offensive line-up. In fact, there are no other team sports in which so much depends on one man as it does on the quarterback in American football. He, in consultation with the team's coaches, decides on strategy, and then, as the man who distributes the ball, is responsible for putting the theory into practice.

American football is very much a game of tactics and strategy – it has been called chess with shoulder pads – and every professional quarterback carries in his head about 200 set plays which the team have practised at great length in training. Before each down he calls the players into a group – known as the 'huddle' – and he tells them which plan of action they are going to adopt on the next play.

Once the quarterback is given the ball by the centre, he steps back 5 to 7 yards and, although there are countless different things he can do on any play, he basically has to choose one of two options. He can either throw the ball to a team-mate who has sprinted off down the field once the ball was snapped, or he can simply put it in the hands of one of his running backs, who line up near him, and they try to burst through the opposite line.

In essence, these are the two ways to gain ground: with a *passing* game, or with a *rushing* (running) game. Obviously, quarterbacks vary their approach between the two during the course of a game – the plays would be too easy for the defense to predict if they stuck to one method – but different teams have different attacking strengths, and naturally place greater emphasis on whichever suits them best.

The success of a quarterback, however, is very much dependent on the frenzied action which takes place in front of him. At the line of scrimmage, members of the offensive team are allowed to block – by shoulder-charging and not by holding – defensive players who in turn are attempting to burst through the line and catch the quarterback before he has time to release the ball. If the quarterback is caught in possession, he is said to have been 'sacked'.

How the Game is Played

If the blockers – the centre, two guards and two tackles who are collectively known as the 'interior linemen' – do their job properly and prevent the defense breaking through, the quarterback has time to look up and assess the situation. The time may be measured only in split seconds but it is long enough for a top quarterback to launch a pass to one of his receivers or to set one of the running backs in motion. He may even decide to run with the ball himself.

In a rushing play, the quarterback makes a very short pass to a running back who has lined up close to him behind the line of scrimmage. The running back attempts to burst through the opposition line, gaps being made for him by his own linemen.

If the quarterback decides to pass, the ball must be thrown from a position behind the line of scrimmage and, although it can be thrown forward, only one forward pass is allowed during a down. As many passes as the offense want are permitted in the course of a down, but only one of them can go forward.

On a passing play, the quarterback can only pass to one of five men on his team, known as 'eligible receivers'. He can pass short to one of the two running backs; he can throw long – and this can often mean a pass of 50 yards or more – to one of his two wide receivers who, as their name suggests, stand out wide at the line of scrimmage and, when the ball is snapped, sprint downfield and move into position to take the catch; or he may pass to the tight end, who lines up next to the tackle at the line of scrimmage and generally makes a block before breaking free to get into a position to catch the ball.

A catch is ruled complete when the ball is in the possession of an eligible receiver who has both feet clearly in bounds. His progress is halted when he is tackled by a member of the opposing team.

The long throw, which is one of the game's most exciting features and which can often bring huge gains of yardage, is a much riskier play than transferring the ball to a running back because there is every chance of the pass being ruled incomplete because it did not go to hand. There is also the possibility of the opposition intercepting. Any member of a defensive team can intercept a pass intended for an offensive player and, providing he catches it cleanly, he can run it back at them, giving possession to his side.

If the ball is thrown and it hits the ground before any player is able to catch it, the pass is incomplete, and play is restarted at the spot where the previous down had begun. The down is lost, so had this happened on first down, the offense would still have 10 yards to make but they would now be on second down. This is called second down and 10.

If on their second down they gained, say, 6 yards, their next play would begin with them still requiring another 4 yards. This would be third down and 4. If they did not make the necessary yardage this time either, they would have one more chance – the fourth down. Then, if they made the ground, the drive would continue with another first down – if they fell short of the target, the ball would pass to the other side.

Very often, when a team reaches fourth down and still has a number of yards to make, they do not take the chance of failing to do so and giving the ball to the opposition in a favourable position. If they are within striking distance of the goalposts, they will attempt a field goal (of which, more later) and if not, they will punt the ball. They bring on the special unit and, as at the kick-off, the punter kicks the ball as high and as far as he can so that, although they have given possession to the opposition, they have given it to them deep in their own territory.

The only other way for the defense to claim the ball – apart from an interception – is if an attacking player who has the ball in control then fumbles it.

When a fumble occurs, there is usually a tremendous scramble for the ball and, if a defensive player comes up with it, possession goes to his side, who now become the offense. Play begins again with their first down at the line where the ball was claimed.

So the four ways for the defense to claim the ball are: by an interception; after a punt on fourth down; when the attacking team fail to make the required yardage on fourth down; or if an attacking player has the ball in his control and then fumbles it.

Otherwise, the *defensive game* is largely one of physical contact, of preventing the opposition from making ground by tackling or blocking them, although strategy comes into play as much for the defense as it does for the offense.

The defense must try to out-guess their opponents and deploy their men to counter the tactics they think the offense will adopt on any given play. For example, if they believe there is going to be an attempt at a rush, they will line up with four men at the line of scrimmage, whose job it is to block the way of the rusher. These four men are two tackles and two ends. In this formation, called the 4–3 defense, three linebackers stand immediately behind them and they react quickly if the team has guessed wrong. They can block the rusher, and they can also drop back to cover the opposition's receivers.

On the other hand, if the defense think the quarterback is going to throw the ball long, they will probably adopt the

3–4 defense. As it suggests, this formation has three men at the line of scrimmage (two ends and a man in the middle called a nose tackle) and four linebackers immediately behind. This gives them more players free to cover the area behind the defensive line of scrimmage, known as the backfield or the secondary, where the offensive receivers will try to catch the pass.

Also covering the backfield in the standard defensive line-ups are two cornerbacks, who stay wide and follow the moves made by the wide receivers, and two safeties, who may be called upon to tackle rushers who have broken through the line or to give additional cover on pass plays. There are many other defensive formations, but these two are the most common.

The countless different permutations for the offense and the defense can, however, make the game look much more complicated than it actually is and, occasionally, it can indeed appear like chess. Mental preparation plays a significant part in a footballer's training, and he can spend as much time in the classroom as on the practice field. He is required to memorize all the moves he, and his team-mates, will make on any set play.

The game's complications make it possible to lose sight of the game's basic objective, to score *points*. Teams can score in one of four ways – by a touchdown (worth six points), a goal conversion after a touchdown (one point), a field goal (three points) or a safety (two points).

Clearly, the touchdown is a team's prime target. A touchdown is awarded when an offensive player catches the ball in, or runs with the ball into, the opposition end zone. If the ball is caught in the end zone, the catcher must have both feet inside the zone. If he jumps to catch the ball, successfully completes the catch, but comes to earth without both feet in the end zone, the touchdown is not allowed. If the ball is outside the end zone but the catcher's feet are inside, the touchdown is given. Unlike a try in rugby, an American footballer does not have to place the ball on the ground in the end zone, but simply has to have it in his possession.

If the ball is run into the end zone, a touchdown is awarded if the player with the ball crosses the line but is then pushed back. There is an imaginary wall extending straight up from the goal line, and if a player breaks through this 'wall' he is credited with the touchdown.

Following a touchdown, the successful team gets the chance to try for a conversion, or 'point after'. For this, the special unit comes on to the field, the ball is snapped back some five yards by the center to a man who holds the ball upright for the team's place kicker to try to kick the ball over the crossbar of the goalposts and between the posts. If successful, he earns his team an extra point.

Exactly the same procedure is adopted for a field goal, which can be attempted from any point on the field and at any time during play. However, it is usually taken on fourth down and is rarely attempted from further than 50 yards from the goalposts. As with the point-after attempt, the defense tries to block the kick, and a successful attempt requires split-second timing and accuracy from the center, the ball holder and, of course, the kicker.

The final, and least common, method of scoring is the safety. A safety is awarded when the defense tackles a member of the offense with the ball behind his own goal line. A safety is also credited to the defense when a member of the offense fumbles the ball in his own end zone, or if an offensive player is guilty of breaking the rules behind his own line. Furthermore, the team which concedes the safety must kick off afterwards, thereby giving up possession, as well as two points, to their opponents.

Clearly, the team with most points after 60 minutes play are the winners. A tied game is settled by sudden-death overtime; often a simple, abrupt action can provide the climax to a plot that has taken 3½ hours to unfold.

2 ATTACKING FORMATIONS

ALTHOUGH an attacking team is required to have seven players on the line of scrimmage, there are countless formations they can adopt – some intended for passing plays, others for running plays. Each professional team has its own playbook, which can contain up to 300 different formations, but some of the more standard, most regularly used, ones are as follows:

THE 'T' FORMATION

This formation, one of the first ever used in the game and revived to great effect by George Halas of the Chicago Bears in the 1940s, is primarily designed for a running play. The quarterback can choose from three running backs and has enough blockers at the line of scrimmage to pave a way for the runner. Because the defensive team are clearly expecting a running play, the quarterback can fool them by opting to pass, although he has only one wide receiver.

'T' FORMATION

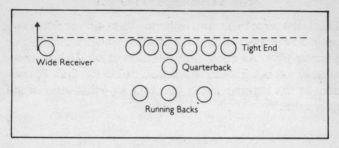

THE 'I' FORMATION

In this line-up, both running backs line up directly behind the quarterback, and this is also a good formation for a running play. The running back at the rear, known as the tailback, is often the one given the ball, and the player in front of him, the fullback, can act as a blocker for him, creating an opening and giving the tailback time to assess the opportunities.

'I' FORMATION

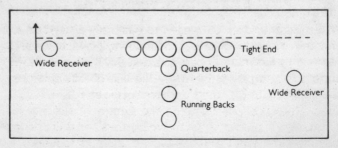

Attacking Formations

THE STANDARD PRO SET

This is the most basic and orthodox formation and has one great advantage – it can be used on either a running or passing play. As such, the defensive team do not know what to expect. This set-up is also called the Split Formation, as the running backs are split on either side of the quarterback.

STANDARD PRO SET

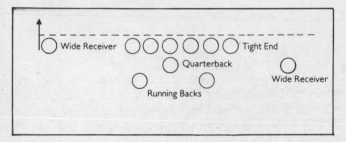

SHORT-YARDAGE FORMATION

When the attacking team need to gain only a yard or so, either for a first down or for a touchdown, it is quite usual to see one of the running backs taking the ball and hurling himself over a pile of bodies at the line of scrimmage to claim the required ground. All seven of the attacking team's linemen are concentrated on the centre of the line of scrimmage to block the defensive linemen and this creates mayhem, over which the ball-carrier attempts to leap.

SHORT-YARDAGE FORMATION

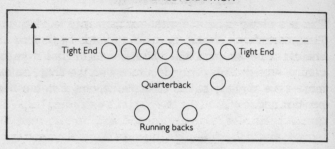

THE TWIN SET

Also known as the slot, this is a formation that gives defensive teams many problems. Although both wide receivers line up on one side, thereby isolating the direction in which the ball can be passed and making coverage by the defense easier, the receivers can act as decoys for each other, running similar patterns and confusing the defense. With this set-up, the attacking team also have the running option, and the running backs can line up as they wish.

TWIN SET

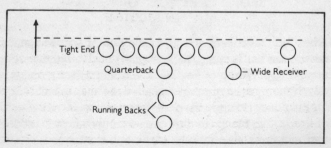

Attacking Formations

THE SHOTGUN

This is a play designed almost exclusively for a pass play. The quarterback stands up to seven yards back from the line of scrimmage and when he receives the ball from the centre, who must be very accurate with the snap, he has more time to study which of his receivers is in the best position and to offload the ball to him. By standing back, the quarterback also has more space and time to read the movements of the defensive linemen. It is a play used quite often when a team has a lot of yardage to make.

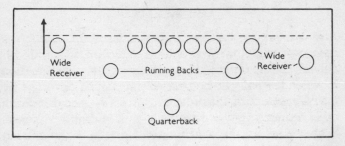

SHOTGUN

MAN IN MOTION

After the teams have set up at the line of scrimmage, but before the ball is snapped, it is quite usual to see one of the attacking players running backwards and forwards, laterally, behind his linemen. He is called the 'man in motion' and his purpose is to keep the defense guessing about the angle of attack. The man in motion can take only one step forward and must run laterally but, as the ball is snapped, he may have moved into a wide position to act as an extra receiver, or he could be switched centrefield to act as a running back or a lead blocker. Often, particularly when a defense is adopting man-to-man coverage, a defending player shadows the man in motion's movements on the other side of the line of scrimmage.

Another way in which the attacking team can fox the defense is by a ploy called 'play action' in which the quarterback fakes giving the ball to a running back and instead steps back and passes it to a receiver.

3 DEFENSIVE FORMATIONS

JUST as the attacking team go into a huddle before each play to decide on which tactics to adopt, so the defensive team do, in an effort to guess what type of play they can expect. There are certain situations in which it is relatively simple to predict what the attacking team will do. For instance, if they have only a short yardage to make, it is reasonable to assume that they will opt for a running play. If they are on, say, third down with 6 yards still to make, they are most likely to pass the ball. Either way, the defense will adopt the formation best equipped to counter the attack they think they will face. Some of the standard defensive formations are described below.

THE 3–4 DEFENSE

This is the defensive formation most commonly used in the NFL. It has three men on the line of scrimmage – a nose tackle, who is directly opposite the attacking team's center, and two ends either side of him – with four linebackers a pace or two behind. Two of the linebackers stand wide of the three linemen (one on either side), while the other two linebackers stand directly behind the linemen. The advantage of this defensive set-up is that it is equally strong against the run and the pass. Essentially, the inside linebackers have the responsibility for containing a running back who may have broken through the line while the outside linebackers, as well as having an eye on a running attack, can also drop back to cover wide receivers. The linebackers must have strength and speed in equal quantities in order to discharge their respective responsibilities.

3 – 4 DEFENSE

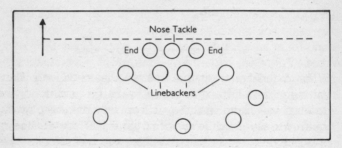

THE 4–3 DEFENSE

The defensive team usually adopt this formation when they are certain that their opponents are going to pass the ball. Two defensive tackles are flanked by two ends on the line of scrimmage and behind them are three linebackers, two outside and one in the middle. With one more lineman than in the 3–4 defense, the defending team have a greater chance of breaking through the attacking line and getting to the quarterback before he has a chance to pass. Because there is one less linebacker, however, they each have to cover a greater amount of ground.

Defensive Formations

4 – 3 DEFENSE

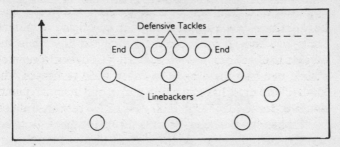

4 – 3 DEFENSE

SHORT-YARDAGE DEFENSE

When faced by an attacking team that need only short yardage for a first down or to reach the end zone, the defense will bring in three or four extra linemen, giving them up to seven on the line of scrimmage. They will line up opposite the gaps between each member of the offensive team and will attempt to counter the surge of the offensive linemen and drive them back. The middle linebacker will be the only defender not directly engaged at the line of scrimmage and his job is to spot where the ball is going and

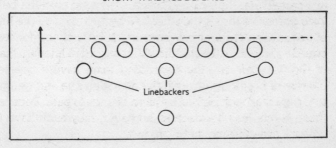

SHORT-YARDAGE DEFENSE

to meet the ball-carrier head-on in an effort to force him back. The defensive linemen adopt very low stances in order to head off the surge of the blockers.

THE BLITZ AND THE DOG

The blitz has one purpose – to sack the quarterback – and is called by the defensive team when they believe the offense are going to pass the ball. In a blitz, the defenders in the secondary – i.e. the cornerbacks and the safeties – rush from their positions in the backfield, break through gaps in the line of scrimmage and collar the quarterback before he passes. Clearly, not all the secondary men take part in the blitz – that would leave no coverage at all in the backfield – but they can rush through alone, in combinations or with the linebackers. It is an unexpected play which puts great pressure on the quarterback. The disadvantage for the defense is that, should the quarterback succeed in passing the ball quickly enough, they lack coverage elsewhere on the field.

THE BLITZ

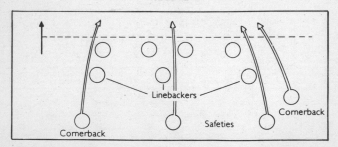

Defensive Formations

THE DOG

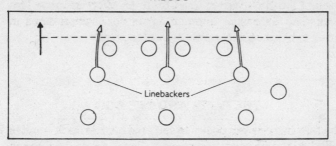

A similar ploy is called a dog. It has the same purpose but in this case it is solely the linebackers who attempt to rush through and surprise the quarterback. Because the dog and the blitz rely on the element of surprise, the defending team must disguise their intentions or the quarterback can switch his tactics to counter the rush.

Defensive plays are usually called by the middle linebacker, who is the defending team's equivalent of a quarterback. He is in the best position to read the play and can change a call at the line of scrimmage based on what he believes the attacking team are going to do.

4 SKILLS

THROWING THE BALL

ONE OF the most exciting sights in American football is that of the quarterback throwing a massive, spiralling pass to be caught by one of his receivers, often 50 or more yards distant, who takes the ball on the run. If successful, such a play always leads to a huge gain in yards for the offense, can often result in a touchdown, and sometimes changes the whole course of a game.

The simplicity with which this move is occasionally completed tends to obscure the fact that there are few more difficult manoeuvres in sport. The quarterback, as well as having terrific nerve to avoid being put off by onrushing defenders, must have amazing judgement and, not least, plenty of power in his forearm and wrist.

The velocity the ball is thrown at is hard for non-players to appreciate, but most sportsmen would find it difficult indeed to catch a ball thrown to them from 50 yards away by a professional quarterback, particularly if they had the attentions of defensive players to contend with as well.

Although each quarterback has his own particular style, they all throw the ball in the same basic way. The ball is gripped towards one end and the fingers are spread out as

Skills

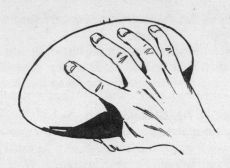

THROWING THE BALL

much as possible so that the last two fingers are stretched over the ball's face.

The quarterback then winds up for the throw. He lifts his arm up and brings it back behind his shoulder, cocked at the elbow, the same preparation for throwing anything a long way.

Having decided on the destination for the ball, he prepares to release. He moves forward and, with his arm still cocked – in the way a gun is before it is fired – he shifts his weight forward and brings his arm up again. With the momentum of his forward movement, his body leans forward and he begins to straighten his arm as it comes level with his head.

He keeps his arm pointing straight at the target and, at the very top of the throw, the gun is fired and the ball is released. As the ball leaves his grasp, his arm is almost perfectly straight.

On releasing the ball, the quarterback flicks his wrist to the inside and propels the ball with his index finger. This gives the ball spin, which helps it to travel faster and truer. A right-handed passer will spin the ball to the right, and a left-handed passer to the left.

With such accuracy, power and nerve required, it is small wonder that the quarterback, who is by no means the most outstanding physical specimen on a team, is usually its star performer.

BLOCKING AND TACKLING TECHNIQUES

There are two main ways of stopping an opponent in American football – by blocking or tackling. Blocking is used by the attacking players either to make room for a running back or to protect the quarterback from onrushing defenders, while tackling is employed by the defensive team to bring to earth the man with the ball.

BLOCKING This is the aspect of the game where brute strength and bulk play the largest part. Even so, agility and speed of thought which give the ability to adapt to a changing set of circumstances are also key ingredients in a good blocker. As soon as the ball is snapped, the defensive linemen at the line of scrimmage attempt to burst through the attacking team's ranks and catch hold of the quarterback before he can release the ball. It is the job of the offensive linemen to prevent this happening.

There are several ways they can do this. A shoulder block is the most common method, the blocker making

BLOCKING

contact with his shoulder and upper arm with a powerful thrust and then continuing to drive his opponent backwards – or at least preventing him from going forwards – with further thrusts. This can create room for a running back.

It is illegal for a blocker to hold an opponent but he can use his hands to fend him off, although he is not allowed to push from behind. Fending-off is usually performed away from the line of scrimmage when the attacking linemen step back to give the quarterback protection on a pass play.

In the open field, when attacking players want to clear the way for one of their runners, the object is to put the defensive player on the ground, not just to block him. To do this, the attacking player charges bull-like at his opponent, keeping his head low and aiming to make the hit at the waist. Providing the timing is correct, the defender has no chance of staying upright.

The other basic method of blocking is employed largely at the line of scrimmage: the offensive lineman keeps his head high and butts his opponent just below the neck, keeping this position to continue to push him away.

TACKLING   Tackling, with which a defensive player halts the progress of an attacking player who has the ball, is essentially the same as it is in rugby, the object being to knock the ball-carrier to the ground.

Technique is not as important as effectiveness but, even so, there are basic, orthodox ways a tackle can be performed, and these are virtually the first things taught a budding footballer. The classic method of tackling is to grab the ball-carrier with both arms round his waist, driving with the legs until he has been put to ground. For more effectiveness, the tackler locks his hands together round the attacker's waist.

Just as important as technique, however, is contact, and even if a tackler cannot put the ball-carrier to ground, he should ensure that he has made sufficient contact with him to slow down his progress, giving team-mates the time to complete the tackle.

Similarly, when an attacking player is running with the ball close to the sideline, a defender should concentrate on knocking him out of bounds by making contact with him, rather than attempting to complete a textbook tackle.

KICKING THE BALL

There are three types of kick employed in American football, and each has its own particular use and requires its own particular technique. The three types of kick are the *punt*, the *kick-off*, and the *place kick* for field goals and extra point conversion attempts.

THE PUNT This is normally used when a team is on fourth down, has a lot of yardage to make to gain a first down and is too far away from the end zone to attempt a field goal. The punter is brought on to the field and his task is to kick the ball as high and as far into the opposition territory as possible. He stands about 15 yards behind the line of scrimmage, ready to catch the ball when it is flicked back to him from the centre on the commencement of the play. He steps forward, drops the ball and kicks it *before* it touches the ground. The kicker uses his instep to kick the ball and the force with which he kicks it takes his foot above head level.

THE KICK-OFF To start, or re-start, the game, one of the teams must kick off. For this, the ball is placed on a small plastic tee and the kicker takes a run up – with the rest of his team following up behind him – and, like the punt, attempts to kick the ball as far and high as he can. Again the instep is used.

Punt

Kick-off

Place kick

Skills

THE PLACE KICK   This manoeuvre is adopted when a team is attempting to score a field goal or to add the extra point for a conversion. It requires a player to hold the ball on the ground for the kicker and demands possibly more accurate timing and split-second execution than any other set play in the game. And although the kicker is the man on whom the main responsibility rests, the center and the holder play a major role in a successful field goal or conversion.

The timing between center, holder and kicker is crucial. As the players line up at the line of scrimmage, the holder moves back 5 yards and crouches with one knee on the ground, his hands outstretched in anticipation of receiving the ball. On a given sign, the centre snaps the ball back to the holder (and the amount of accuracy required in this manoeuvre should not be underestimated), the kicker begins his two-pace run-up, the holder catches the ball, holds it upright for the kicker who, if the timing is right, kicks the ball without any disruption to the rhythm of his run-up.

The holder, who is often a quarterback, must be a good handler of the ball and used to pressured situations. He must make sure that the ball's lace is pointing away from the kicker, the whole sequence of actions taking just more than a second.

The kicker approaches the ball from a sideways angle and kicks the ball with the instep and top of a slightly out-turned foot. As with the other types of kick, he must try to keep his eyes looking downwards as long as possible while following through with his foot.

5 ALL ROADS LEAD TO THE SUPER BOWL

THERE are twenty-eight professional football clubs in America who make up the National Football League. The clubs are authorized, or franchised as it's known, by the NFL to take part in the league. They are divided into two leagues – known as conferences – of fourteen teams each. These are the National Football Conference and the American Football Conference, and they are further split into three divisions each, two of five clubs and one of four.

The divisions in each conference are organized on a broadly geographical basis. Unlike soccer in Britain, the divisions in American football are not related to the standards of the teams involved.

Each conference has an Eastern, a Western and a Central Division, and the set-up is as follows:

AMERICAN FOOTBALL CONFERENCE

Eastern Division	*Western Division*
Buffalo Bills	Denver Broncos
Indianapolis Colts	Kansas City Chiefs
Miami Dolphins	Los Angeles Raiders
New England Patriots	San Diego Chargers
New York Jets	Seattle Seahawks

All Roads Lead to the Super Bowl

Central Division
Cincinnati Bengals
Cleveland Browns
Houston Oilers
Pittsburgh Steelers

NATIONAL FOOTBALL CONFERENCE

Eastern Division
Dallas Cowboys
New York Giants
Philadelphia Eagles
St Louis Cardinals
Washington Redskins

Western Division
Atlanta Falcons
Los Angeles Rams
New Orleans Saints
San Francisco 49ers

Central Division
Chicago Bears
Detroit Lions
Green Bay Packers
Minnesota Vikings
Tampa Bay Buccaneers

The season lasts for twenty-one weeks between September and January, and the goal of every team is to win the Super Bowl, American football's equivalent of the Cup Final. The Super Bowl is played between the champions of each of the two conferences and the winners are called 'World Champions'.

But before they arrive at that stage, teams must complete a programme of sixteen matches in what is known as the regular season. The most successful teams over the regular season qualify for a series of play-offs that reaches its climax with the Super Bowl. In its simplest form, the American football season is a league programme culminating in a knock-out competition.

In the regular season, each team plays every other team

in their own division twice, home and away. The balance of their sixteen-game schedule is made up of some fixtures against teams within the same conference and between two and four games against opposition from the other conference. This arrangement gives supporters the chance to watch the star players from the rival conference and adds to the variety in a team's fixture list.

Working out the fixtures is a complicated business. A team never has the same opposition in successive seasons, and an elaborate formula decides which teams they meet from the other conference. This is largely decided by the previous season's placings and, as far as possible, the fixtures are planned so that all the teams in any division play the same opposition from the rival conference.

The divisions are just like any other league tables, and the winners are the team with the best record, which is expressed in terms of matches won and lost. For example, if it is said that a team is '12 and 4', it means that they have won twelve and lost four of their regular season matches.

STRUCTURE OF NFL COMPETITION

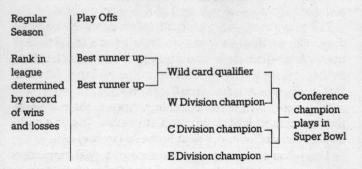

On completion of the regular season, each conference holds its play-offs to arrive at the champion club which will go on to contest the Super Bowl. The teams involved in the play-offs are the winners of the three divisions and two other teams from the conference who have the best records without finishing on top of any of the divisions.

When the top two teams in a division have identical won-and-lost records, the place in the play-offs goes to the team that has a better record in matches they played against each other during the season. If this fails to decide matters, it falls to the team with a better record in games within the division, and if this still cannot break the tie, the team with a better record in games within the conference is given the verdict.

Similar rules apply when two teams who have not won a division are competing for a place in the play-offs as the best runners-up. When two teams from separate divisions have identical records, the team which has a better record in matches between the two goes forward. If they did not play each other during the season, it is decided on the better record in games within the conference.

Either way, the play-off series begins with a match between the conference's two best runners-up. They contest the right to go further as a 'Wild Card' qualifier.

The winners of the wild-card eliminator join the three divisional winners for two matches that are, in effect, the conference semi-finals. The winners of these matches play in the conference championship game and the victors of that match go forward to the Super Bowl.

In the play-offs, home advantage goes to the team with the better record over the regular season. The wild-card team, however, never play at home in the play-offs.

There has only been one instance of a wild-card team going on to win the Super Bowl (the Oakland Raiders in 1981) but, more recently, the New England Patriots lost in the 1986 Super Bowl after qualifying as a wild card.

The Puffin Book of American Football

The Super Bowl venue changes each year and is decided upon three years in advance. It is therefore possible for a team to be playing on their home ground in the Super Bowl but, in the 21-year history of the competition, this has never happened.

The present format for professional football in America has only been in existence since 1970, following a long and often bitter period of rivalry between the National Football League and the American Football League. In 1966 they agreed to a merger under the umbrella of the NFL but decided to postpone the move until 1970.

The two former leagues were re-titled 'conferences', and at the time they joined forces there were thirteen teams in each. Since then, Seattle Seahawks and Tampa Bay Buccaneers have joined the league, both in 1976.

The first Super Bowl was played on Sunday, 15 January 1967, at the Los Angeles Coliseum and was a result of the new-found spirit of fellowship between the two leagues. It was played between the champion club from each league: the Green Bay Packers beat the Kansas City Chiefs 35–10.

It was entirely appropriate that the Packers, who were then the nation's most exciting and powerful team, should have launched an event that was soon to become America's most popular and important sporting occasion.

At that time – before the two leagues had merged – the match was called the 'World Championship', but by 1970 'Super Bowl' had been adopted as its title. The new name was suggested by Lamar Hunt, owner of the Kansas City Chiefs, who is believed to have thought of the title seeing his daughter play with a toy rubber 'super ball'.

Desperate to give a historical feel to what is essentially a new phenomenon, the history of the Super Bowl is counted in Roman numerals. By the time the New York Giants met the Denver Broncos in 1987, we had reached Super Bowl XXI.

All Roads Lead to the Super Bowl

But even for such a recently created event, there is a great deal of folklore attached to the Super Bowl. The Green Bay Packers won the first two Super Bowls – both by large margins – but the solid silver trophy they won was later to have painful significance for the club.

In 1969, the man who had coached them to their triumphs, Vince Lombardi, died. In recognition of his outstanding achievements, both as a coach and earlier as a player with the New York Giants, the Super Bowl trophy was immediately re-christened the Vince Lombardi Trophy.

The trophy itself is a fitting memorial to Lombardi. It is 20 inches high, weighs seven pounds and represents a regulation-size football mounted on a three-sided column.

It is customary for the winning club in a Super Bowl to present each of their players with a ring to commemorate the achievement. This ring, often encrusted with diamonds, is usually worth several thousand pounds and adds to the prize money won by a Super Bowl victor.

For their triumph over the New England Patriots in Super Bowl XX, each Chicago player received $36,000 (£25,000 at that time), with every player on the losing side earning half that amount. The total prize fund for the two competing clubs was more than $2·5 million (£1·7 million).

The main reason the players earn such handsome rewards is that the Super Bowl itself generates an enormous amount of money. Tickets, which are almost impossible to get, cost upwards of £50 and can go for many hundreds on the black market; a 30-second advertisement during the television transmission of the match costs about $1 million; and the sale of souvenirs can produce an amount of money that would solve the financial problems of some third-world nations. Super Bowl XX injected more than $100 million (£70 million) into the New Orleans economy, with the travelling fans spending an average of £170 each per day.

New Orleans has been lucky enough to host the Super Bowl on six occasions, more than any other city. Next come Miami with five and Pasadena with four.

One of the features of the Super Bowl is the pre-game and half-time entertainment, and a great deal of money and resources are poured into presenting a spectacular live show. With each Super Bowl, the show becomes more spectacular.

The half-time presentation lasts 15 minutes and, at the 1986 game, more than 500 performers from twenty-two countries put on an extravaganza which involved a sophisticated light show and a revolving stage which occupied almost a quarter of the pitch.

Everything about the Super Bowl is on a grand scale. It is one of the few events that unites America, and it is entirely in keeping with the event that the President often makes a live broadcast to congratulate the champions.

The television coverage of the game surpasses every other single sporting event in the world. To cover Super Bowl XX in New Orleans, NBC (one of the two biggest broadcasting companies in America) sent along three match commentators and a production crew of 120, operating twenty-one cameras. They also had fourteen video-tape machines which provided action replays of the game from every angle.

The size of the television audience demands this blanket coverage. Super Bowl XX was watched on TV in America by 127 million viewers, the largest TV audience in history. Of the six television presentations to have attracted more than 100 million viewers, five are Super Bowls.

In addition to its audience in the United States, the match was televised in fifty-nine other countries, including live coverage in Britain. It was even watched by an estimated 300 million when highlights were screened in China.

6 FROM RUGBY SCHOOL TO SUPER BOWL

IT MAY be difficult to believe, but the sport of American football has its origins in an English public school of the early 1800s. The modern game, with its high technology and razzmatazz, may seem to belong more to the space age, but its development owes much to an incident at Rugby School in the autumn of 1823.

It was then that William Webb Ellis, a sixth-form pupil at the school, disregarded the rules of the crude football game played by the students, picked up the ball instead of kicking it, and ran with it towards the opposition goal line.

That single event sparked the birth of rugby union, which Britain was to give to many nations throughout the world, and also had its repercussions in America, where soccer was the major sport.

Soccer in America had developed on similar lines to Britain, where it had grown from 'mob football' – an unruly ball game between gangs of men, usually from different towns, that dated back to the Middle Ages. Colonists had taken this pastime across the Atlantic with them and it was so rough that, in 1657, the city fathers of Boston banned it.

The great colleges of the north-east of America – Harvard and Yale – kept the practice going with ritual matches but, as in England, the game gradually became more cultured with the advent of a ball that encouraged dribbling and passing. By the mid-1800s, the development of soccer was well under way.

Two colleges, Princeton and Rutgers, began the tradition of inter-college sport on 6 November 1869 with a game, loosely based on soccer, in which each side had 25 players. Rutgers won 6–4, and the first college rivalry was established.

However, the trend towards rugby was now growing and Harvard became the first college to adjust the rules and adopt a handling game. This became known as the 'Boston Game', but the men of Harvard had no one to play against.

In 1874, they organized a match, under compromise rules, against McGill University of Canada, where fifteen-man rugby had already taken root. The game was a great success, and it encouraged other colleges to follow the fashion.

Yale, Princeton and Rutgers all began to play this new game, even though there was a good deal of confusion over the rules.

Soccer remained popular among the students, and a match between Yale and Eton College of England in 1873 was, strangely, a key factor in the growth of American football. On the touchline was a Yale student, Walter Camp, whose imagination was fired by the open, fluent style of the game. He was quick to see how some of soccer's rules could be adopted to make the brand of rugby being played more attractive.

What made the biggest impression on Camp was soccer's eleven-a-side format. He felt that reducing the numbers in rugby from fifteen to eleven would ease congestion on the field and help the game flow. He also thought it was unfair to have a competition to win the ball in a scrummage (as in rugby), and instead he suggested that when a team's progress is halted, play should re-commence with the two teams lined up in formation while an attacking player heels back the ball to a colleague.

These proposals, put forward at a convention in 1876, were adopted by the colleges, and American football, in a form that could be recognizable today, was born. Not surprisingly, Walter Camp is regarded as the father of the sport.

A decade of development followed, with the rules undergoing many refinements. By 1900, the game was on almost totally different lines from rugby, with only the oval-shaped ball and the goalposts remaining from the original sport.

Camp, by now coach of the Yale side, was the instigator of most of the changes, and it was one of his innovations in 1888 that, briefly, was to alter the nature of the game. He introduced a rule which made it legal for a player with the ball to be tackled below waist height but above the knees (previously a tackle could only be made above the waist). This had the obvious effect of making tackling much easier, and teams now put the accent on defence. Open running suddenly became more difficult and, as a result, the game was far less attractive.

Furthermore, this new rule led to a tactic – known as the 'Flying Wedge' – whereby the attacking team charged down the pitch in a 'V' shaped formation, with the man holding the ball at the sharp end of the 'V' leading the surge towards the opposition. Would-be tacklers were left in their wake, causing untold injury.

The wedge, and other such massed formations, made the game much more savage, and led to a great deal of violence on the pitch. The wedge was banned in 1894 but similar tactics were still implemented and the brutality persisted, and even got worse. By 1905, the violence had reached such a level that the President of America had to step in.

In one season, eighteen players were killed and 159 seriously injured on the field of play, and President Theodore Roosevelt instructed the colleges to clean up football or he would ban it. As a result, the representatives of the colleges formed the National Collegiate Athletic Association and set about reforming the game.

They outlawed any formation resembling the wedge, brought in a new points-scoring system (six points for a touchdown, one for a conversion and three for a field goal), allowed an attacking team four plays to make 10 yards and, perhaps most important, made the forward pass legal. It says much for their wisdom that all these rules have survived to the present day and were crucial early steps in making American football the spectacle it is today.

At that time, the sport was still primarily a college pursuit, but soon athletic clubs throughout America began to take up football. The move towards professionalism had started.

There was great rivalry between the athletic clubs no matter what sport they were competing in, and nowhere was the competition more intense than in the city of Pittsburgh, Pennsylvania. Two of the city's clubs, the Allegheny Athletic Association (AAA) and the Pittsburgh Athletic Club (PAC), challenged each other to a football game and, as they were deadly rivals, there was a vast amount of local pride at stake.

The match, played on 12 October 1892, ended in a 6–6 draw, and the hostilities grew more bitter when it was discovered that PAC had played a man who was not a member of the club. A month later, the clubs met in a re-match and now it was AAA's turn to field non-members.

From Rugby School to Super Bowl

Included in their side was William 'Pudge' Hefelfinger, a former star of the Yale side, and he scored the only touchdown in a 4–0 victory for his side.

But Hefelfinger's place in history was more than simply as a match-winner; he was paid $500 for turning out for AAA, thus becoming the sport's first professional player.

A row raged over the payment of players, but soon other athletic clubs followed suit and professionalism on a large scale had arrived (baseball had been professionalized as early as 1871).

The top footballers hawked themselves around and were available to the highest bidder. There were no organized leagues as teams sprang up in the states of New York, Philadelphia and Illinois, yet although the game's structure was haphazard, crowds were attracted to the matches and attendances of 4,000 and upwards were the norm.

However, college football was still the major attraction and, while the crowds for the professional game were healthy enough, they paled in comparison to those for the big college matches. For instance, the first Rose Bowl, played between the all-conquering Michigan University and Stanford, was watched by 20,000 fans.

Ill-fated attempts were made to form professional leagues, and a 'World Series' involving four clubs lasted only two years (1902–03). The popularity of pro football declined in its birthplace, Pittsburgh, and some of the top players moved to the Massilon Tigers of Ohio, the state which now became the game's stronghold.

By 1904, Ohio had at least eight professional teams, and bidding for players was cut-throat to say the least. The Massilon Tigers and their arch-rivals, the Canton Bulldogs, were the two most powerful teams of the day, and matches between them (which were referred to as 'championship' games) were fiercely contested.

They also attracted much betting and, in 1906, a newspaper alleged that the Canton coach, Blondy Wallace, had attempted to fix the result of a game to win a wager. Wallace never admitted the allegation but none the less quit Canton under a cloud, leaving behind the sour smell of scandal.

This incident set back the game's progress, interest in both cities dipped and, for almost a decade, football stagnated. But in 1915 the greatest college player of the day joined the professional ranks and the crowds flooded back to watch him.

Jim Thorpe was possibly the finest athlete of his generation, a college footballer of some repute, and a double gold medallist in the 1912 Olympics (in pentathlon and decathlon). His decision to join the Canton Bulldogs – at the phenomenal fee of $250 a game – gave football revived momentum.

Canton, with Thorpe and several other talented players in their ranks, were almost unbeatable, and their reputation helped to rekindle interest in the game. Once more, teams began to spring up, and football now needed an organized league to prevent it from falling fallow again.

The key meeting was held in the unlikely surroundings of a car showroom in Canton in September 1920. Representatives from clubs in four states – Indiana, Ohio, Illinois and New York – sat on the bonnets and running boards of the cars and thrashed out their ideas.

The outcome of the meeting was the formation of the American Professional Football Association, with each club to pay a membership fee of $100. No club ever paid the fee and, in its first year of operation, the league was somewhat disorganized. No records of the matches were kept and three clubs – Akron, Buffalo and Canton – all claimed the championship.

Yet this first season represented a landmark in more ways than one. Bob Nash, a defensive tackle, became the first club player to be sold when he joined Buffalo from Akron for the princely sum of $300.

By the time the 1921 season started, the new league had taken a very important step in appointing Joe Carr as president. Carr, a strong willed, energetic champion of the cause, was to remain in office over two decades. He quickly tightened up the organization and, although college football still attracted the main public interest, the new league began to emerge as a credible force.

The Chicago Staleys (who became the Bears the following year) were declared champions in 1921, a season which had seen the arrival of the Green Bay Packers. The league expanded even further in 1922 and, in keeping with its lofty ambitions, adopted the name it has today – the National Football League.

One of the new clubs, the Oorang Indians, recruited the great Jim Thorpe but, finishing with one win and ten defeats, they folded after just one season. Clubs came and went during the NFL's early years but the Canton Bulldogs remained all-powerful. In 1924, now based in Cleveland, they won their third consecutive championship.

The game desperately needed personalities, however, and one arrived, with devastating effect, in 1925. Red Grange had earned his nickname 'The Galloping Ghost' with his remarkable exploits as a running back in college football and was, by some margin, the most popular player of the day.

In 1925, with the University of Illinois season over, Grange agreed to join the Chicago Bears for a fee that would make him a rich man. It also made money for the Bears as 38,000 spectators paid to watch Grange play against the Chicago Cardinals.

With Grange, by now a national figure, in their side, the Bears undertook a tour of America that did much to spread the popularity of professional football. They played nineteen games in sixty-six days, the highlight being a match against the recently-formed New York Giants which drew a crowd of 73,000. With an ambitious manager behind him, Grange then demanded a five-figure salary and a third share in the ownership of the Bears. This was rejected, and Grange and his manager, C. C. Pyle, went off to form their own league. Like other later attempts to rival the NFL, it had only a brief existence, folding in 1927.

A year later, Grange was lost to football, deciding on a career in acting. But he returned to the Bears in 1929, helped them to win two NFL championships and then retired at the end of the 1934 season at the age of 32.

By this time, the league had split into two five-team divisions, with the winners of each meeting to decide the championship. In 1935, the system of drafting college players was introduced, with the club who finished in last place in the league the previous year having the first pick of the college talent.

The game was developing well – although the rules often appeared complicated and caused many controversies – but an era ended with the death in 1939 of Joe Carr, who had steered the NFL through its birth pains to relative prosperity. The year was also marked by the first television coverage of a game, between the Brooklyn Dodgers and the Philadelphia Eagles.

From Rugby School to Super Bowl

By the time the nation had emerged from the Second World War, the NFL had another threat to its supremacy. The All American Football Conference was established in 1946 and, unlike other such offshoot leagues, the standard of football in the AAFC was high, and it did produce one outstanding team, the Cleveland Browns. With a membership of eight clubs, the AAFC lasted four seasons, all of which were dominated by the Browns.

In 1950, a merger was arranged between the two leagues, with three AAFC clubs – the Browns, the San Francisco 49ers and the Baltimore Colts – joining the NFL. The Browns emphasized just how good they were by winning the NFL championship in their first season.

The game was now becoming more and more popular, with TV taking the action into a growing number of living rooms. The Los Angeles Rams were the first club to have all their matches televised, and others soon followed suit. In 1951, the championship game was broadcast coast-to-coast for the first time, and football had become truly national.

The security which long-term television contracts gave the NFL was needed, however, to meet the challenge of yet another rival league. Under the leadership of Texan oil millionaire Lamar Hunt, the American Football League was set up in 1960, with eight teams – mainly from places without NFL teams – playing in two divisions.

The NFL, aware of the serious threat, expanded to include clubs in Dallas and Minnesota, and these proved to be the first shots in a war that was to last six years. At its height, both leagues spent vast amounts of money to persuade the top college players to join them.

The AFL was very much the junior organization, but crowds were healthy and they managed to secure a lucrative TV deal. Yet, in competition with each other, both leagues were set on a collision course that might have spelled disaster for each. So, for reasons of commercial sense, they agreed to combine in 1966, forming a unified league of twenty-six teams. The merger was not to take place until 1970 but, as from 1967, the two league champions were to meet in an end-of-season title game modestly called the 'World Championship'.

The Green Bay Packers of the NFL won the opening championship, with the New York Jets, led by their great quarterback Joe Namath, becoming the first AFL representative to take the prize, in 1969. For the fourth in the series in 1970, the game became known as the Super Bowl, a title suggested by Hunt.

When the leagues finally joined forces in 1970, Baltimore, Cleveland and Pittsburgh agreed to join the AFL teams and form the American Football Conference while the thirteen remaining NFL teams would make up the National Football Conference. The conferences were split into East, West and Central divisions, and the champions of each conference played in the Super Bowl, this being how the NFL currently operates.

The addition of one team in each conference – Seattle in the AFC and Tampa Bay in the NFC – in 1976 brought the NFL to its present size of twenty-eight clubs.

The game continued to prosper, with the Super Bowl becoming America's most popular single sporting event, watched by capacity crowds and, by 1986, more than 100 million television viewers. To add to the end-of-season jamboree, the league established the Pro Bowl, a match played after the Super Bowl between all-star sides representing the AFC and the NFC. The tradition remains, with selection being a great honour for any player. The game is now played in Hawaii.

From Rugby School to Super Bowl

Further attempts by other organizations to cash in on football's popularity have gone the same way as most of their predecessors. The World Football League, set up in 1974, lasted just a season, while the USFL, with big-money backing and some highly regarded college players, folded in 1986 after failing to attract sufficient crowds.

Perhaps the biggest threat to the NFL's well-being came in 1982 when the players went on strike during the season. The strike, over pay, lasted fifty-seven days and was ended when the clubs' owners agreed to a minimum salary for players and doubled team members' play-off bonuses

The season ended with only nine regular season games completed out of a programme of seventeen, and a play-off format involving sixteen teams was adopted. Following the strike, the NFL brought in a rule limiting clubs to a playing staff of forty-nine.

Since then, the game has got bigger – if not necessarily better – and in 1985 attendance records were broken when 902,000 fans bought tickets for one weekend's matches. In 1986, more than 13 million spectators watched the season's games and, for the NFL, those early, hesitant years must seem more than just a century away.

ATLANTA FALCONS

National Conference, West Division
Ground: Atlanta-Fulton County Stadium, Atlanta
Capacity: 60,748   **Surface:** Grass
Colours: Red, black, silver and white
Championships: Division, 1980

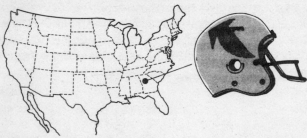

The Falcons were founded in 1966 by Atlanta businessman Rankin M. Smith, who paid more than $8 million for the franchise. He is still chairman of the club, and with his sons as president and secretary, the Falcons are very much a family concern. Indeed, when Smith established the club, it was registered under the name of 'Five Smiths Incorporated'.

The NFL Clubs

Their relatively short time in professional football has not been particularly sweet. Their rivals in the West Division of the National Conference are the San Francisco 49ers, the Los Angeles Rams and the New Orleans Saints, making it one of the most competitive divisions in the NFL. The Rams and the 49ers are traditionally strong teams and only once, in 1980, have the Falcons managed to finish at the head of the division.

The Falcons have nevertheless made it to the play-offs as a wild-card qualifier on two other occasions (1978 and 1982), but luck has never been with them in the play-offs, where they have lost by agonizingly small margins.

Yet their early days promised much. In their debut season, they shocked the football world by claiming their first victory in New York at the expense of the mighty Jets. This was immediately followed by a triumph over the St Louis Cardinals and, so it seemed at the time, a great team was born.

Other successes followed, but it was not until 1971 that the Falcons finished a season winning more games than they lost. The club continued to progress steadily until they appeared to be on the verge of a big breakthrough in 1973. In the first game of the season, the Falcons annihilated New Orleans 62–7 in what remains the club's most successful afternoon. They then proceeded to win their next six games, but a poor ending to the regular season cost them a place in the play-offs.

This has been the way of the Falcons so far – a lot of promise but with little achieved.

One of the club's most successful players has, strangely, been an Englishman. Mick Luckhurst, from St Albans, joined the Falcons as their kicker and, despite missing the occasional field goal, built up a reputation as one of the most reliable kickers in the game. In 1984 he became the Falcon's all-time leading scorer and, together with wide receiver Billy 'White Shoes' Johnson, is one of the most notable figures to have worn the red helmet of the Falcons.

The NFL Clubs

BUFFALO BILLS

American Conference, East Division
Ground: Rich Stadium, Buffalo
Capacity: 80,000   **Surface:** Artificial
Colours: Scarlet, royal blue and white
Championships: Division, 1980; AFL, 1964, '65

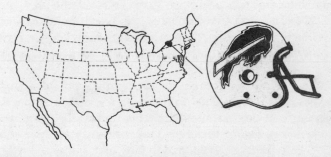

The Bills were one of the original members of the American
Football League when it began in 1960. Their founder was
Ralph C. Wilson Jr, who set up in Buffalo when his plans to
establish a team in Miami were thwarted. Named after
William Cody, the original Buffalo Bill who claimed to have
killed 4,000 buffaloes, the team have never enjoyed lasting
success.

Their most productive years were in the mid sixties when
they won the AFL Championship two years in succession,
narrowly missing a hat-trick.

They were, however, responsible for producing one of
the greatest talents the game has ever seen. O. J. Simpson,
known as 'The Juice', joined the Bills in 1969 from college
football, and in his eight-year spell at Buffalo he became
one of the most successful running backs in the league. His
first two seasons gave few indications of what he was to

achieve, but in 1972 he ran for more than 1,000 yards and was elected the AFC Player of the Year. Still, this was little in comparison to the following season when he rushed for more than 2,000 yards, breaking a record which had stood for more than a decade.

But one man does not make a team and, even with the remarkable Simpson in their ranks, the Bills were seldom anything other than also-rans. They did reach the play-offs in 1974 as a wild-card qualifier only to be overwhelmed by the Pittsburgh Steelers. Their reliance on Simpson was such that if the opposition defense could work out a way to stop him, the Bills had no answer.

When Simpson retired to concentrate on an acting career in 1977, the Bills suffered an inevitable setback, winning only three games that season. But by 1980 they had gone some way to restoring their pride by winning the AFC East Division, even though they lost in the play-offs. They made the play-offs again the following year as a wild card but lost once more. Since then, the Bills have virtually sunk without trace and in 1984 won only two of their sixteen games.

Hope arrived at Buffalo in 1986 in the shape of their new quarterback Jim Kelly, who had been playing in the rebel USFL. The Bills paid a huge fee for Kelly and their investment was partly repaid on his first home appearance. The Bills had been having difficulty in filling half the seats at Rich Stadium but the arrival of superstar Kelly brought in an 80,000 capacity crowd for the opening game of the season.

The NFL Clubs

CHICAGO BEARS

National Conference, Central Division
Ground: Soldier Field, Chicago
Capacity: 65,790   **Surface:** Artificial
Colours: Orange, navy blue and white
Championships: Division, 1984, '85, '86; Conference, 1985;
Super Bowl, 1985; NFL, 1921, '32, '33, '40, '41, '43, '46, '63

The man who became known as 'Papa Bear', George Halas,
was more than just the founding father of the Chicago Bears:
he was a key figure in establishing professional football
itself. Halas played a leading role in the meeting in 1920
which set up the American Professional Football Association.

His team – the Decatur Staleys, sponsored by the Staley
starch-manufacturing company – were one of the original
members of the league. Two years later, Halas had bought
out the Staleys, moved them to nearby Chicago and, because they shared their ground with the Cubs baseball
team, re-named the team the Bears.

Halas went on to be head coach of the Bears for a total of
forty years in four ten-year spells between 1920 and 1967.
He was largely responsible for making the professional
game popular, and it was not long before it rivalled the

college game for public interest. The major factor in this was Halas's signing of the phenomenal college star Red Grange before the Bears embarked on an action-packed 66-day tour of the States.

A crowd of 73,000 turned up at New York to watch Grange, who became a national figure. A row over his salary ended with Grange leaving the Bears in 1926 but he was back three years later and eventually retired from playing in 1934. Grange inspired the Bears to win the NFL championship in 1932 and 1933.

The club's most glorious era came in the forties when they earned the nickname 'The Monsters of the Midway'. In 1940 they took their fourth NFL championship, annihilating the Washington Redskins 73–0, and followed this up by taking the title a further three times in the following five years.

The 1946 championship was to be the Bears' last major success for seventeen years, during which time Halas retired as coach, only to return in 1958.

Halas led the club out of this transitional period, and in 1963 the bruising Bears beat the New York Giants to win their eighth NFL title. In 1968, Halas retired as head coach for good; aged 73, his record over four decades was an astonishing 320 wins, 147 defeats and 30 draws.

The Bears suffered an understandable hangover from Halas's departure, and in 1969 they had their poorest season for almost fifty years – one win in fourteen games.

It wasn't until 1984 that the Bears showed signs of being roused again. They won their division and, with the direction of coach Mike Ditka and the huge talent of running back Walter Payton, the Bears were Super Bowl bound the following season.

They were by far the game's most powerful team in the

The NFL Clubs

1985 season – as their record of fifteen wins, one defeat shows – and nobody was able to prevent them winning their first Super Bowl. They took the prize by demolishing the New England Patriots by the record score of 46–10.

CINCINNATI BENGALS

American Conference, Central Division
Ground: River Front Stadium, Cincinnati
Capacity: 59,754 **Surface:** Artificial
Colours: Black, orange and white
Championships: Division, 1970, '73, '81; Conference, 1981

When the Bengals joined the American Football League in 1968, they appointed as their head coach Paul Brown, who had already coached the Cleveland Browns to seven Championship victories and was regarded as one of the best tacticians in the game. It was hardly a surprise that under his direction the Bengals made an immediate impact.

They won their first match (at home to Denver) and, in only their third year in existence, they made the play-offs. Even though they then lost to Baltimore, the Bengals were established, and Brown felt he could ease into an administrative role; he is still the club's general manager.

His good work on the coaching side was carried on by Homer Rice, who led the club to their second divisional title in 1973. But after a number of largely unsuccessful seasons, Rice made way for Forrest Gregg in 1979, and the downward spiral was quickly halted.

The NFL Clubs

Working with very limited resources, the club, now playing in their familiar tiger-stripe helmets and uniform, took the 1981 divisional title, winning twelve of their sixteen matches. They went on to defeat San Diego in the most horrendously cold conditions (the wind chill factor was −59°F in Cincinnati that day) to claim their first Conference title and a place in the Super Bowl against the San Francisco 49ers.

The Bengals were very much the outsiders and, when San Francisco led 20–0 at half time, the forecasts looked justified. But a stirring second-half fightback by the Bengals (roared on by their mascot, an Indian white tiger) almost brought them a most unlikely victory. The 49ers clung on to win 26–21, but had the Bengals not made a series of crucial errors, the prize might have been theirs. Nevertheless, the second-half performance of veteran quarterback Ken Anderson remains one of the most exciting in Super Bowl history.

The Bengals were back in the play-offs the following season when a players' strike meant that only nine regular-season games were played. The Bengals lost only twice before going down heavily to the New York Jets in their first play-off game. Since then, the Bengals have struggled to achieve any consistency but are never to be taken lightly.

CLEVELAND BROWNS

American Conference, Central Division
Ground: Cleveland Stadium, Cleveland
Capacity: 80,000   **Surface:** Grass
Colours: Seal brown, orange and white
Championships: Division, 1971, '80, '85; NFL, 1950, '54, '55, '64; AAFC; 1946, '47, '48, '49.

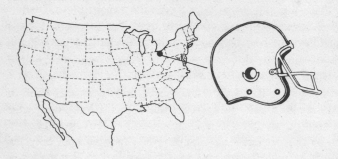

At the end of the Second World War, Cleveland was left without a football team. The Cleveland Rams, who had joined the National Football League in the early 1930s, decided to become the first club on America's west coast and moved out to Los Angeles.

Cleveland businessman Arthur McBride filled the gap by establishing a new team which, in 1946, entered a new league (the All American Football Conference) which had been set up as a rival to the NFL. McBride offered a prize of $1000 to the fan who came up with the best name for the new club. He was deluged by suggestions, and by far the most popular was 'Browns' after the club's head coach, Paul Brown.

The name was adopted and Brown became the only man in the game to have his team named after him. If there was any doubt that Brown would repay the faith of the fans, this was quickly removed. No team has ever made such an immediate impression. They won every championship in the four-year existence of the AAFC with a total record of forty-seven wins, four defeats and three ties.

When the AAFC disbanded in 1949 and the Browns joined the NFL, their record was scarcely any poorer. In eight years, they contested the championship game seven times, and were victorious on three occasions.

In 1953, McBride sold the club for the massive sum of $60,000, and the new owners were quick to realise the force behind the Browns' success: they took out a huge life insurance policy on Paul Brown.

Coincidentally, it was another Brown who was soon to take over as the hero of Cleveland. Jim Brown was a star running back in college football, and in 1957 he exploded on to the professional scene with Cleveland. In only his fourth game, Brown rushed for a record 237 yards in a game, and a legend was born. He continued to tear apart the opposition that season and was deservedly named Rookie of the Year.

In eight years with the Browns, Brown broke nearly every record in the game before settling for a somewhat less hazardous occupation as a film star.

The Browns have never been able to recapture their all-powerful form of the late forties and early fifties when they were feared throughout the land. In 1971, 1980 and 1985, they finished top of their division, but these proved to be false dawns as the Browns suffered convincing defeats in the play-offs. They were then pipped by the Denver Broncos for the AFC title in 1986.

DALLAS COWBOYS

National Conference, East Division
Ground: Texas Stadium, Irving
Capacity: 63,749   **Surface:** Artificial
Colours: Royal blue, metallic blue and white
Championships: Division, 1970, '71, '73, '76, '77, '78, '79,
'81, '85; Conference, 1970, '71, '75, '77, '78; Super Bowl,
1971, '77

With an NFL record of twenty consecutive winning seasons, including eighteen appearances in the play-offs and
two Super Bowl triumphs, the Cowboys are traditionally
one of the hardest teams in the game to beat.

Their head coach is, and always has been, the great Tom
Landry, who has been at Dallas since the club started in
1960 and, in the period up to 1986, had an all-time winning
record second only to George Halas of the Chicago Bears.
Landry started the team from scratch, picking his players
from other NFL teams, and has always been original in his
approach to the game.

In 1962, he invented the 'shuttling quarterback offense'
which saw the team's two quarterbacks taking the field for

alternate plays. It paid dividends with four victories in eight games but injuries disrupted the team's plans. However, having lost eleven and tied one in their first season of competition, the Cowboys were definitely on the upgrade.

It was in 1966 that the Cowboys began to reveal their true power and, over the following twenty-one seasons, they missed the play-offs only three times. They ended the 1966 season with a record of ten wins and three defeats, going on to play the Green Bay Packers for the NFL championship. In one of the most exciting title games ever, the Packers eventually won 34–27 and doubled the agony for the Cowboys the next year when they repeated the triumph on one of the coldest days on record at Green Bay – minus 13°C.

On both occasions the Packers went on to win the Super Bowl, but the Cowboys soon took over as the game's most regular visitors to the big game. They endured Super Bowl defeat in 1970 when a field goal nine seconds from the end gave the Baltimore Colts victory, but the very next year the Cowboys were back to erase the memory of that defeat. Indeed, they convincingly lost their tag as the side who were always likely to lose on the big occasion by defeating the Miami Dolphins 24–3 in Super Bowl VI.

Four years later the Cowboys were back at the Super Bowl but, despite leading for much of the match, were beaten 21–17 by the mighty Pittsburgh Steelers. Again the Cowboys did not have to wait long before putting things right. In Super Bowl XII, their defense hounded the Denver Broncos to defeat, the Cowboys winning 27–10.

Their fifth visit to the Super Bowl – more than any other club – came the following year (1978) when, in a thrilling game, they were beaten 35–31 by the Steelers. It was at this time that the Cowboys promoted themselves as 'America's Team', a title which has stuck since.

The player who had a vital role in most of their successes, quarterback Roger Staubach, retired in 1980 after 11 record-breaking seasons, but still the Cowboys continued to win. However, in 1984 they failed to reach the play-offs for the first time in a decade.

The NFL Clubs

DENVER BRONCOS

American Conference, West Division
Ground: Mile High Stadium, Denver
Capacity: 75,100   **Surface:** Grass
Colours: Orange, blue and white
Championships: Division, 1977, '78, '84, '86; Conference, 1977, '86

The Broncos were one of the founder members of the American Football League in 1960 and, in their early days, were distinctive only by playing at a stadium a mile above sea-level and by having vertically striped socks. The socks were the subject of much controversy – hated by the supporters and many of the players – and in a public ceremony before the 1962 season they were ritually burned in the hope that this might provide the Broncos with good luck.

However, in the same division as tough teams like the Oakland Raiders, the Los Angeles Chargers and the Dallas Texans, the Broncos needed more than just kind fortune. By the mid sixties, with a series of poor seasons behind them, the Broncos were in trouble. Crowds fell dramatically and the club was up for sale. Yet when a broadcasting company announced that they were about to buy the club in order to move it to Atlanta, the supporters rallied round to keep the Broncos in Denver. Attendances were quickly on the increase again and the future of football at Mile High Stadium was secured.

Success on the field was never achieved with such ease, and the story of the Broncos is a slow rise towards respectability. But by 1977 they were strong enough to win their competitive division, and victories over Pittsburgh and the LA Raiders gave them the Conference Championship and a place in the Super Bowl. They were never in with a chance against the might of the Dallas Cowboys, however. The Cowboys were in their meanest mood and their 27–10 victory reflected their superiority.

Still, the Broncos had arrived as a force, and to show that their Super Bowl appearance was not a fluke, they won their division again the next year, thanks largely to their defensive line, which became known as the 'Orange Crush'.

From such uncertain beginnings, the Broncos became a tough team to beat and, in 1983, they had to be taken even more seriously when, in one of the biggest player deals ever, they bought the star young quarterback John Elway from Baltimore. It is believed that Elway's fee was $6 million for a five-year contract. Elway's early performances were just as unmemorable as those of the Broncos themselves, but he also grew in stature gradually and, in 1984, led them to a third divisional championship before taking them to Super Bowl XXI, where they did not have enough firepower to overcome the New York Giants.

DETROIT LIONS

National Conference, Central Division
Ground: Pontiac Silverdome, Michigan
Capacity: 80,638 **Surface:** Artificial
Colours: Honolulu blue and silver
Championships: Division, 1983; NFL, 1935, '52, '53, '57

Until 1934, the club had existed under a number of different names and had been in at the very start of organized professional football in 1920. The Heralds, the Panthers, the Wolverines and finally the Portsmouth Spartans had been forerunners to the Detroit Lions who, once formed, became one of the game's powers.

They won the first ten matches of their initial season in 1934 (preventing their opponents from scoring on seven occasions) and followed this up by claiming the National Football League championship the following year.

After all the time it took the club to establish themselves, they had at last shown they were to be regarded as serious contenders. Major problems off the field – which saw the club bought and sold at regular intervals in the early years – were miraculously survived, and in 1947 a group of local businessmen seized control of the Lions; they finally settled down to become one of the strongest teams in the league.

In 1952 they won the NFL championship again by beating the great Cleveland Browns on their own ground. Throughout the fifties, the Lions were the only consistent threat to the dominance of the Browns and won the championship on two more occasions, in 1953 and 1957.

After seven lean seasons, the club was sold once more in 1964, but still performances continued to slump. Even the efforts of such people as Charlie Sanders, one of the best offensive blockers the game has ever known, and defenders of the calibre of Alex Karras and Lem Barney, failed to bring the Lions further success.

The club have always had big ideas, and in 1976 they moved out of town to the newly-built Silverdome at Pontiac, the largest domed stadium in the world. Their new home was only a short distance away from the city of Detroit but, from their early nomadic existence, the Lions had, in most respects, come a long way.

Still, the impressive new surroundings were not sufficient to bring about an upturn in the club's plunging fortunes on the field. It was not until the 1980s that there were any signs that the Lions were ready to roar again. As wild-card qualifiers, they made the 1982 play-offs, and the following season they took the NFC Central Division, only to be beaten by one point by San Francisco in the play-offs.

GREEN BAY PACKERS

National Conference, Central Division
Grounds: Lambeau Field, Green Bay, and Milwaukee Stadium
Capacity: 56,189 (Lambeau Field) 55,958 (Milwaukee Stadium)   **Surface:** Grass
Colours: Green and gold
Championships: Division, 1972; Super Bowl 1966, '67; NFL, 1929, '30, '31, '36, '39, '44, '61, '62, '65, '66, '67

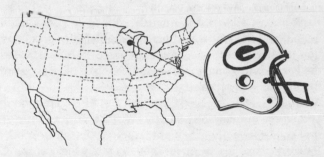

From their humble beginnings in 1920 as the works team for the Acme Packing Company in Green Bay, the Packers grew into the most successful club in the history of pro football. Ten NFL championships and victory in the first two Super Bowls give them a record second to none, even if they have failed to match these feats since the NFL and the AFL merged in 1970.

Two of the great figures of American football dominate the Packers' history. Earl 'Curly' Lambeau was one of the founders of the club and, both on and off the field, he inspired their all-conquering performances of the thirties. Some thirty years later, Vince Lombardi took over as head coach and led the club to even more success.

There was never much doubt that the Packers were destined for greatness. In their very first season in 1920, they won ten out of eleven games, and, even though they were beset by problems brought on by lack of money and too much bad weather, they were one of the most feared teams when they joined the National Football League in 1921.

They had to wait until 1929 before winning their first championship but, under Lambeau's direction, they claimed the top prize in the next two seasons as well and were almost invincible for a decade.

The great days were to return in the sixties. In 1959, the Packers signed Vince Lombardi of the New York Giants as coach, and he soon set about re-establishing their reputation. In 1960, Lombardi, voted Coach of the Year, steered the Packers to a divisional championship. This was to prove the first of many triumphs.

In 1961, 1962 and 1965 they won the NFL championship, and when, in 1966, the champions of the NFL and the AFL met in the title game that was to become the Super Bowl, the Packers were again successful, beating the Kansas City Chiefs 35–10. This remained the highest margin of victory in the Super Bowl for seventeen years.

The Packers were almost unbeatable, and it was only right that the following season they won Super Bowl II, defeating the Oakland Raiders 33–14. They have never returned to the Super Bowl since, but the mark made by the Packers was recognized when the Super Bowl trophy was named after Vince Lombardi on his death in 1969.

The mighty Packers have fallen from grace recently – with only a divisional title in 1972 to lift the gloom – but their history remains one of the richest in the game, and they can claim to be the only club with the same name, and in the same town, as in 1921 when the league was formed.

The NFL Clubs

HOUSTON OILERS

American Conference, Central Division
Ground: Houston Astrodome
Capacity: 50,496   **Surface:** Artificial
Colours: Columbia blue, scarlet and white
Championships: Division, 1967; AFL 1960, '61

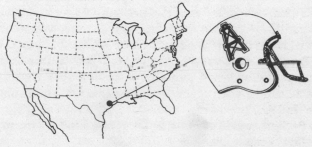

The Oilers have been mainly unsuccessful in recent years, and are one of the few teams in the league who regularly fail to sell out tickets for their home games. All this is in sharp contrast to their highly promising beginnings in 1959, when they were founded by Texas oilman Bud Adams.

In their first season, the Oilers won the AFL championship. With veteran quarterback George Blanda – who had been signed from the Chicago Bears – at the helm, the Oilers beat the Los Angeles Chargers in the title game. The next season, the same teams met to decide the championship again and, although the Chargers had by now moved to San Diego, the outcome was the same.

On their way to the title, the Oilers had won ten successive matches and, in scoring 513 points in the regular season, became the first team to score more than 500 points.

In 1962 they won the AFL's eastern division for the third

year in a row, winning eleven of their fourteen games. But after overtime in the AFL championship game, they lost 20–17 to the Dallas Texans. This traumatic defeat left its mark on the Oilers, who have never been a force in the game since.

Just two seasons after the loss to Dallas, they finished bottom of their division, with four victories to ten defeats. They continued to struggle throughout the sixties, and their only other divisional title – in 1967 – was immediately followed by a 40–7 thumping by the Oakland Raiders in the play-off game. The decade ended with the Oilers suffering another humiliating defeat by the Raiders again, this time by a margin of 56–7, and little better was to follow in the seventies.

When the leagues were amalgamated, the Oilers were pitched in with the Pittsburgh Steelers and the Cleveland Browns in the AFC Central Division, and things went from bad to worse. In the 1972 season, the Oilers won only one game (remarkably against the great New York Jets) and scored only 164 points during the campaign.

Events were no more encouraging off the field, and in 1974 the Oilers announced a loss of £½ million. The only change in their misfortunes came in 1978 when, as a wild card, the Oilers qualified for the play-offs, beating the New England Patriots before losing heavily to the Pittsburgh Steelers, the eventual Super Bowl champions. History was to repeat itself the following year when the Oilers qualified as a wild card and again lost to the Steelers.

INDIANAPOLIS COLTS

American Conference, East Division
Stadium: Hoosier Dome, Indianapolis
Capacity: 60,127   **Surface:** Artificial
Colours: Royal blue, white and silver
Championships: Division, 1970, '75, '76, '77;
Conference, 1970; Super Bowl, 1970; NFL, 1958, '59, '68

Nobody could accuse the Colts of failing to keep on the move. They began life as the Miami Seahawks, re-surfaced in Baltimore as the Colts and then moved on to Indianapolis in March 1984.

Their chequered history has seen its share of success, although not in their guise as the Seahawks. The Seahawks were members of the ill-fated All American Football Conference and by 1946 had declared themselves bankrupt. The franchise was taken to Baltimore where they were re-named the Colts.

When the AAFC was disbanded in 1950, the Colts joined the NFL, but two years later the club had reached its lowest ebb. With only two regular-season wins behind them, the Colts decided to call it a day. But after two years without a football team, the Baltimore public agitated for the club to be revived.

Their pleas were noted by the commissioner of the NFL, who said that Baltimore would be granted the franchise again if 15,000 season tickets could be sold in six weeks. The target figure was reached with time to spare and, in time for the 1953 season, the Colts were back in business and were soon to enjoy a remarkable period of success.

Under coach Weeb Ewbank, the Colts won the NFL championship in 1958 and 1959, both times at the expense of the New York Giants. In the Colts team was Johnny Unitas, whom many regard as the best quarterback the game has ever seen, and Raymond Berry, who went on to become coach of the New England Patriots.

In 1963, Don Shula (later to become the highly successful coach of the Miami Dolphins) took over at Baltimore and led the club to a record eleven consecutive victories in 1964. The 1968 season saw the Colts make it to the Super Bowl, but they were beaten by the New York Jets. However, they made up for this disappointment two years later by beating the Dallas Cowboys 16–13 in Super Bowl V, clinching victory with a field goal five seconds from time.

The Colts, despite frequent divisional titles since, have never threatened to return to the Super Bowl, and they are still looking to establish themselves in Indianapolis after their traumatic move from Baltimore. They received a tremendous welcome from the people of Indianapolis – 143,000 season-ticket requests were received when the club hit town – but in their first two seasons at the Hoosier Dome, the Colts won just nine of their thirty-two games.

KANSAS CITY CHIEFS

American Conference, West Division
Stadium: Arrow Head Stadium, Kansas City
Capacity: 78,067   **Surface:** Artificial
Colours: Red, gold and white
Championships: Division, 1971; Super Bowl, 1969;
AFL, 1962, '66, '69

The Chiefs are owned by Lamar Hunt, the Texan multi-millionaire who was one of the founding fathers of the AFL, helping to establish six AFL teams.

The Chiefs started life in 1960 as the Dallas Texans and, unlike their great rivals, NFL club Dallas Cowboys, they were an immediate success. The Texans never had the popular support enjoyed by the Cowboys, but they made up for it by winning the AFL championship in 1962, beating Houston in a highly exciting game that went into overtime.

Because the Texans failed to attract the crowds in Dallas, Hunt gratefully accepted an offer from the mayor of Kansas City to move the club. In 1963, they re-emerged as the Chiefs and quickly set about winning over the fans in their new home.

They began brilliantly, beating Denver 59–7, but unfortunately this proved to be the highest point for some time. By the end of the 1964 season, after two mediocre years, there were persistent rumours of the Chiefs moving on again. Hunt resisted the temptation to close down the ailing club, and his faith was rewarded by a gradual upturn in the team's performances, which culminated in their reaching the first Super Bowl in 1967.

The Chiefs were no match for the mighty Green Bay Packers, but they had at least arrived as a force. This fact was confirmed at the end of the 1969 season when, in Super Bowl IV, they beat the Minnesota Vikings 23–7 after few people had given them a chance.

Now settled in Kansas City, the Chiefs moved in 1972 to their new home in Arrow Head Stadium, a vast futuristic arena with a capacity of just over 78,000 which cost $73 million to build. Their impressive new surroundings, however, failed to spur the Chiefs on to repeat their triumphs and, since winning the Super Bowl, the cupboard has been bare.

In 1981, the Chiefs won more games than they lost for the first time since 1973 but, by 1985, they had slumped again, finishing at the foot of their division with a record of six wins and ten defeats.

The NFL Clubs

LOS ANGELES RAIDERS

American Conference, West Division
Stadium: Los Angeles Memorial Coliseum
Capacity: 92,516   **Surface:** Grass
Colours: Silver and black
Championships: Division, 1970, '72, '73, '74, '75, '76,
'83, '85; Conference, 1976, '80, '83; Super Bowl, 1976, '80,
'83; AFL, 1967

Since 1963, when Al Davis took over the struggling Oakland
Raiders with a pledge to transform them into a successful
football club, the Raiders have had the best won–lost
record in the game.

The club had been born in Oakland, California, in 1960
and, although they had a few promising players, rarely
looked likely to trouble any of the established teams. A
move across the bay to San Francisco did little to improve
matters, as their 1962 record of one win and thirteen defeats
testified. But, on returning to Oakland in 1963, things were to
improve dramatically with the arrival of Davis, who was
both head coach and general manager.

He adopted as the club's motto 'Commitment to Excel-
lence', and performances since clearly indicate that the
Raiders followed his watchwords. Eight divisional titles,

three conference championships and three Super Bowl triumphs have been the Raiders' haul; and they have not had a losing season since 1964.

In 1982 Davis took the Raiders from unfashionable Oakland in search of bigger crowds, and the move to the Los Angeles Coliseum, where the 1984 Olympic Games were held, was certainly well supported. In 1983, the Raiders attracted the biggest ever crowd for an AFC Championship game (more than 92,000) when they beat the Seattle Seahawks, before going on to win Super Bowl XVIII by defeating the Washington Redskins by a record margin of 38–9.

This was the third time the Raiders had lifted the Super Bowl trophy. They had already claimed their place in the game's history in 1980 by becoming the first team to win the Super Bowl after qualifying for the play-offs as a wild card. The Raiders' defense, renowned as one of the toughest in the game, were particularly formidable in the Super Bowl, where they beat Philadelphia 27–10. The Raiders' other Super Bowl triumph came at the end of the 1976 season, with Minnesota the victims.

A string of brilliant players have worn the famous silver and black colours of the Raiders, including running back Marcus Allen, voted the Most Valuable Player in Super Bowl XVIII and the NFL's top-rated rusher in 1985. The man who helped engineer many of the Raiders' triumphs was Tom Flores, who was the club's quarterback in the early days at Oakland and went on to become head coach.

The NFL Clubs

LOS ANGELES RAMS

National Conference, West Division
Stadium: Anaheim Stadium, California
Capacity: 69,000   **Surface:** Grass
Colours: Royal blue, gold and white
Championships: Division, 1973, '74, '75, '76, '77, '78, '79, '85; Conference, 1979; NFL, 1945, '51

The Rams were the first club to establish a home on America's west coast. Until 1946 they were the Cleveland Rams, but they moved west in search of a kinder climate and a more prosperous environment. This they found in Los Angeles, yet, while the Rams built up a reputation as one of the game's most popular teams, their record was somewhat disappointing.

Throughout the fifties, they had a team to match everyone but managed to win only one NFL championship, in 1951. Similarly, in the seventies they won their division in seven successive seasons yet made it as far as the Super Bowl just once, losing to Pittsburgh 31–19.

Even though they have recently been overshadowed by the Raiders, the Rams have always had glamour and talent, and by winning their divisional title in 1985 (their first for six years) they gave notice that they are not yet ready to be cast in the role of poor neighbours. However, the trophy cabinet has been empty since 1951 (when, ironically, they beat Cleveland for the NFL championship), as the Rams have failed to achieve the consistency to go with their undoubted potential.

Just four years after winning the NFL title, they were in the play-offs again, but this time Cleveland gained their revenge. As if to illustrate the unreliable nature of the team, the Rams then finished bottom of their division the following season with four wins and eight defeats.

It was not until 1967 that they returned to winning ways. They took the NFL Coastal Division (as it was then called) with only two defeats to their name but were beaten by the all-conquering Green Bay Packers in the play-offs. The Rams played second fiddle to San Francisco in the NFC West Division when the leagues were merged in 1970, but by 1973 they had established a stranglehold that was to last until 1979.

Seven divisional titles on the trot ended with the unsuccessful visit to Super Bowl XIV at nearby Pasadena. In 1980, the Rams moved to Anaheim Stadium, home of the Los Angeles Dodgers baseball team, but as yet have failed to end their trophy famine. If encouragement were needed, it arrived in 1983 in the shape of running back Eric Dickerson who, in his first season, broke the NFL rookie rushing record, as well as five club records along the way. In 1984 he went on to break the legendary O. J. Simpson's season rushing tally of 2,003 yards and is firmly set to be one of the best runners of all time.

MIAMI DOLPHINS

American Conference, East Division
Stadium: Orange Bowl, Miami
Capacity: 75,206 **Surface:** Grass
Colours: Aquamarine, coral and white
Championships: Division, 1971, '72, '73, '74, '79, '81, '83, '84, '85; Conference, 1971, '72, '73, '82, '84; Super Bowl, 1972, '73

In 1965, life-long football fanatic Joseph Robbie paid $7½ million for the Miami franchise, and the Dolphins, thus named after a contest which drew 20,000 entries, were born. Robbie was soon to discover that starting a football team from scratch was no easy job and, in the first four years of their existence, the Dolphins won fifteen and lost thirty-nine of their matches.

It was in 1970 that the club began to take off. Amid much controversy, Robbie lured Don Shula from Baltimore, where he had earned a reputation as one of the cleverest coaches in the business, and immediately the Dolphins began to reverse their losing trend.

The season before Shula arrived at the Orange Bowl, the Dolphin's record was won three, lost ten; Shula's first year ended with a total of ten wins, four losses.

Thereafter, the Dolphins have never looked back, and since the AFL–NFL merger in 1970 they have the best won–lost record in the league. They have also made five appearances in the Super Bowl and in 1972 established a record that has yet to be equalled: they won every game they played, culminating in a 14–7 victory over the Washington Redskins in the Super Bowl. It was a perfect season, in every respect.

The Dolphins then went on to repeat the achievement of the Green Bay Packers by winning the Super Bowl in successive years; this time the Minnesota Vikings were their victims.

Shula was later voted, deservedly, coach of the decade for the seventies. His strict discipline and tactical genius have kept the Dolphins on top in the eighties as well, and they came close to a hat-trick of Super Bowl triumphs in 1983 when, leading with 10 minutes remaining, they were eventually beaten 27–17 by the Redskins.

That year an equally important event took place off the field, when the Dolphins signed quarterback Dan Marino from the University of Pittsburgh. In his second year, Marino set season records for passes completed and touchdown passes. Marino led the Dolphins to the best record in the NFL – won fourteen, lost two – and they reached the Super Bowl as warm favourites. However, the predictions were wrong as the Dolphins were beaten 38–16 by the San Francisco 49ers. Despite a bad start to the 1986 season (the first time the Dolphins have won only one of their first five games since Shula took over) Marino is set on a course that seems certain to lead to the Hall of Fame.

The NFL Clubs

MINNESOTA VIKINGS

National Conference, Central Division
Stadium: Hubert Humphrey Metrodome, Minneapolis
Capacity: 62,212   **Surface:** Artificial
Colours: Purple, gold and white
Championships: Division, 1970, '71, '73, '74, '75, '76, '77, '78, '80; Conference, 1973, '74, '76; NFL, 1969

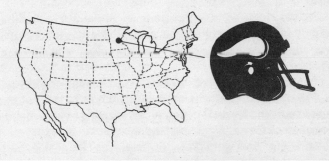

The 'nearly men' of American Football, the Vikings have little to show for a record of consistency that has few equals. Between 1969 and 1983, the Vikings reached the play-offs eleven times and played in four Super Bowls, only to lose on each occasion and establish an unenviable record of unsuccessful Super Bowl visits.

Only twice in the seventies did they fail to win their division and the defense, known as 'The Purple Gang' or 'The Purple People Eaters', were feared throughout the game. But, as their record suggests, the Vikings were something of a let-down when it came to the big game.

The club was formed in 1960 and, with a collection of cast-offs and has-beens, they were given very little chance of survival. They finished their first season of competition with three victories, and although this failed to send tremors through the football world, it was a creditable start all the same.

Only two games were won the following season but, by 1964, the Vikings had established a platform from which they were to dominate their division in the seventies. They won eight of their fourteen games in 1964 and, even though it was another four years before they again had a winning season, the Vikings now had to be taken seriously.

But the club had to suffer traumas off the field, resulting mainly from a rift between head coach Norm Van Brocklin and the quarterback, Fran Tarkenton. Relations between the two almost broke down completely before Tarkenton issued an ultimatum that either the coach went, or he went.

The drama ended with them both going and the Vikings were soon on an even keel again. By winning twelve of their fourteen games in 1969, the Vikings won their division for the first time and went on to represent the National Conference at the Super Bowl. However, they were beaten 23–7 by Kansas City, and defeat in the Super Bowl was an experience they were soon to become used to.

The bitterness of their four Super Bowl losses – which all came in the space of eight years – seemed to have its effect on the Vikings and, in 1979, the club endured its first losing season for twelve years. Although they came back to claim the divisional title the following year, they have since been overtaken by the Chicago Bears as the division's strongest unit.

While luck has rarely been on their side, the Vikings remain a team capable of beating the best on their day, and they gave a perfect illustration of this midway through the 1986 season when they inflicted on the mighty Bears their first defeat for almost a year.

The NFL Clubs

NEW ENGLAND PATRIOTS

American Conference, East Division
Stadium: Sullivan Stadium, Foxboro
Capacity: 61,279   **Surface:** Artificial
Colours: Red, white and blue
Championships: Division, 1978, '86; Conference, 1985

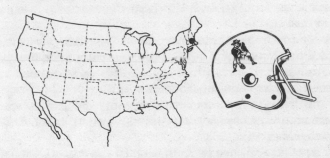

When the American Football League was established in 1960, the last of its eight franchises was given to Boston. It was not until 1971 that the Boston Patriots moved out of town to what was then called Schaefer Stadium, Foxboro, to become the New England Patriots, and it was not for another seven seasons that a significant triumph was claimed, the Patriots winning their division in 1978.

Things did indeed move slowly for the Patriots, even though they won more games than they lost in four of their first five seasons. Beset by financial problems in their early days – they lost $300,000 in the first year – the Patriots were never able to match the successes of Boston's baseball team, the Red Sox, and thus big crowds were difficult to attract.

It was hoped that the move out to Foxboro would see the dawn of a new era for the Patriots, and they received a further boost when the highly promising college quarter-back Jim Plunkett was drafted that same year.

However, Plunkett, despite his obvious talent, never settled with the Patriots, and after five largely unsuccessful seasons, he joined the Oakland Raiders and went on to become one of the most highly regarded quarterbacks in the game. Plunkett was followed by Steve Grogan and at last the Patriots seemed to have discovered a winning formula.

Under Grogan's leadership, the Patriots narrowly lost the wild-card qualifier in 1976 before, two years later, the club finally took away a prize, winning the divisional title but then losing to Houston in the play-offs.

In their highly competitive division, the Patriots continued to go close until they fell apart in 1981, winning only two games all season.

It has been a steady climb back for the Patriots since. In 1983 – the year their stadium was renamed Sullivan Stadium in honour of the club's owner – the Patriots made it to the play-offs, but their greatest, and most unexpected, triumph came two years later when, as a wild-card qualifier, they reached the Super Bowl.

They may have been demolished 46–10 by the vastly superior Chicago Bears, but their achievement in reaching the Super Bowl ranks as one of the most outstanding in the game's history. In each game in the play-offs – against the New York Jets, the LA Raiders and the Miami Dolphins – they had to play away from home and were rank outsiders. But coach Raymond Berry plotted their unlikely route to the Super Bowl before reality – and the Bears – caught up with them.

NEW ORLEANS SAINTS

National Conference, West Division
Stadium: Louisiana Superdome
Capacity: 71,647   **Surface:** Artificial
Colours: Old Gold, black and white
Championships: None

The club's nickname – the New Orleans Ain'ts – tells its own story. Formed in 1967, the Saints have never reached the play-offs and indeed have never even had a winning season. Their best regular season record was eight wins and eight defeats in 1979 and 1983. In the 1980 season, they had to wait until the last but one game before claiming their one and only victory of the year, and then by only a 21–20 margin.

Yet their beginnings had been very promising. Their very first game against the LA Rams was watched by more than 80,000 fans in Tulane Stadium, and the kick-off was returned 94 yards by a Saints player for a remarkable touchdown. Even though the Rams went on to win the match, the baptism was a highly encouraging one.

Six more games came and went before the Saints claimed their first victory, and they ended that initial campaign with two more wins under their belt.

The 1970 season yielded only another couple of victories but saw the Saints earn a place in the record books when their kicker, Tom Dempsey, who had no right hand and no toes on his right foot, kicked the longest field goal in the game's history. It measured an astonishing 63 yards.

Nevertheless, failure followed failure for the Saints, and in 1975 they moved to the Louisiana Superdome, the largest indoor stadium in the world. But the change of surroundings did not bring a change of fortune: when coach Joe North was fired following a succession of poor results, the Saints were looking for their fourth head coach in only ten years.

A gradual improvement was brought about by the quarterback Archie Manning, and in 1979 the Saints' won–lost record was even for the first time.

The hapless Saints were put up for sale in 1984 and, as if to prove that there is always someone who has faith, they were bought by Tom Benson for the staggering sum of $70 million. Benson has yet to receive the return on his investment, although it has to be said that the Saints' divisional opposition includes both San Francisco and the LA Rams, daunting enough for the best of teams. Yet, in the NFL, most teams get a turn at the top – and the Saints' is still to come.

The NFL Clubs

NEW YORK GIANTS

National Conference, East Division
Stadium: Giants Stadium, New Jersey
Capacity: 76,891   **Surface:** Artificial
Colours: Blue, red and white
Championships: NFL, 1927, '34, '38, '56; Division, 1986;
Conference, 1986; Super Bowl, 1986

Of the two New York teams, the Giants have the history and
the tradition, having been in existence since 1925 when, in
the early days of the sport, it was felt essential to establish a
team in America's most important city.

At that time, the citizens of New York were interested
only in baseball but, from the moment football was launched in the city, their passions were divided.

The club was set up by an Irishman, Timothy J. Mara, who
paid just $2,500 for the franchise. A key factor in the sport's
immediate impact in New York was an exhibition game
Mara arranged between the Giants and the nation's most
exciting team, the Chicago Bears.

In the Bears' team was running back Red Grange, known
as the 'Galloping Ghost' and renowned throughout the
country. A crowd of more than 70,000 saw the Bears win, but

the game was exciting enough to persuade sizeable numbers of New Yorkers to follow the Giants in their formative years.

They did not need too much encouragement as, in their first season, the Giants won eleven of their twelve games to win the NFL championship. They followed this up with further titles in 1934 and 1938, although there were times during the period of depression in the thirties that the club came close to folding.

The 1956 season proved to be a landmark for the Giants; they moved from the Polo Grounds to Yankee Stadium (home of the baseball team) and celebrated by winning their fourth NFL title. With Frank Gifford (now a television presenter) in the side, the Giants crushed their old rivals, the Chicago Bears, 47–7 in the championship game.

Strangely for a club with such heritage and pedigree, this proved to be the Giants' last major success until 1987. They have continued to produce many outstanding players and have been something of a breeding ground for coaches. The great Vince Lombardi of the Green Bay Packers and Tom Landry of the Dallas Cowboys were both at one time on the Giants' staff.

Between 1956 and 1963, the Giants lost four NFL championship games, and in all they have been runners-up on thirteen occasions. Since then, the Giants made the playoffs as wild-card qualifiers in 1984 and 1985, but they had to wait until 1987 to emulate their great rivals, the Jets, in winning the Super Bowl, overcoming the Denver Broncos in Pasadena.

The NFL Clubs

NEW YORK JETS

American Conference, East Division
Stadium: Giants Stadium, New Jersey
Capacity: 76,891   **Surface:** Artificial
Colours: Green and white
Championships: AFL, 1968; Super Bowl, 1968

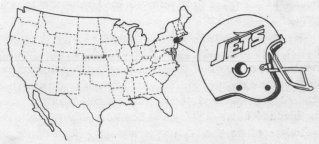

The Jets were one of the original members of the American
Football League in 1960, although in those days they went
under the name of the New York Titans. Unlike the Giants,
they failed to make an impact early in their history, and it
was not until 1963 that the Titans began to emerge as a
significant force.

Struggling to attract crowds, they were near bankruptcy
when, on 28 March 1963, a group of New York businessmen
bought the club for $1 million, renamed the team the Jets,
and persuaded the brilliant Weeb Ewbank to leave Baltimore and take over as coach at New York.

An even more important off-the-field event took place
the following year when they managed to get the services
of Alabama college quarterback Joe Namath. Even though
Namath had a problem with a knee injury, his presence
transformed the Jets, and he set them on a course that was
to end with a glorious Super Bowl victory.

In Namath's first season, in 1965, he was voted the AFL's Rookie of the Year, and his superstar status meant that all the Jets' home games at Shea Stadium were sold out. With Namath, known as 'Broadway Joe', the Jets reached Super Bowl III, where they faced the powerful Baltimore Colts, who had lost only one regular season game and were hot favourites to take the big prize.

Namath, in a blaze of publicity, guaranteed to their fans that the Jets would win the Super Bowl, and his forecast was proved right as they overcame the odds to win 16–7 and become the first team from the AFL to win the Super Bowl.

The following year the Jets reached the play-offs again, but defeat by Kansas City ruled out a return to the Super Bowl. Despite the arrival of a magnificent running back, John Riggins (later to be a star with the Washington Redskins as well), the Jets never led the pack again.

Namath's knees continued to trouble him, and in 1971 he spent more than three months on the sidelines. He returned to claim more records and strike up a fine partnership with Riggins, but the Jets failed to reach the play-offs again until the strike-shortened 1982 season.

By then, Namath had retired after spending a fruitless eight months with the LA Rams and had been replaced as a cult figure by a defensive end called Mark Gastineau. The Jets defense became known as the 'New York Sack Exchange' because of their ability to catch opposing quarterbacks in possession. Gastineau's celebratory jig – the 'Sack Dance' – became legendary.

Rivalry with the Giants is as fierce as ever, even though the two clubs share the same ground. The Jets moved from Shea Stadium to take up joint occupation of Giants Stadium in 1984.

PHILADELPHIA EAGLES

National Conference, East Division
Stadium: Veterans Stadium, Philadelphia
Capacity: 71,640 **Surface:** Artificial
Colours: Green, silver and white
Championships: Division, 1980; Conference, 1980;
NFL, 1948, '49, '60

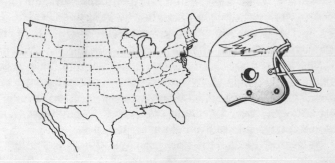

One of the senior clubs in the game, the Eagles have had a turbulent history. They entered the league in 1933 when the franchise belonging to the once-successful Frankford Yellowjackets was transferred to the Eagles after a change in the law made it possible to play sport on a Sunday in Philadelphia.

The Eagles struggled for ten years and in 1943 merged with the Pittsburgh Steelers to become known as the 'Steagles'. That experiment lasted only one season, and when the Eagles assumed their own identity again, they began to establish themselves as a power.

Starting in 1944, they finished runners-up in their division three years in succession before going one better in 1947. They were beaten by the Chicago Cardinals in the championship game but returned for revenge the next season, defeating the Cardinals for the championship in a match played in an appalling snowstorm.

The Eagles were now almost unstoppable, and in 1949 they completed a hat-trick of divisional titles, going on to repeat their championship triumph and ending the season with twelve victories and only one defeat.

The fifties were barren for the Eagles in a division that fell under the domination of the Cleveland Browns. But the Eagles surfaced again in 1960 when they pipped Cleveland for the divisional title and then beat Green Bay 17–13 in an exciting match for the championship.

Another slump was to follow – in 1962 and 1963 they finished bottom of the division – before a gradual upturn in their fortunes led to the club being valuable enough in 1969 for Leonard Tose, a haulage contractor, to pay what was then a record sum of $16 million for the club.

He moved the club to a new ground at Veterans Stadium, but the team's results were disastrous. In 1972, the Eagles won only two matches and were set for a long period in the wilderness.

By reaching the wild-card qualifier in 1978 and 1979, the Eagles gave notice that they had a successful team in the making, and they proved this in 1980 by winning the National Conference – conceding fewer points than any other team – and going on to Super Bowl XV to meet the Oakland Raiders, who had become the only wild-card team to go all the way to the big game.

The Eagles were confidently predicted to win but, by making countless elementary errors, they handed victory to the Raiders. Since then, the Eagles have failed to come out on top of their division, although the arrival of new head coach Buddy Ryan from Chicago in 1986 gave the Eagles a reason to look optimistically at the future.

The NFL Clubs

PITTSBURGH STEELERS

American Conference, Central Division
Stadium: Three Rivers Stadium, Pittsburgh
Capacity: 59,000 **Surface:** Artificial
Colours: Black, gold
Championships: Division, 1972, '74, '75, '76, '77, '78,
'79, '83, '84; Conference, 1974, '75, '78, '79; Super Bowl,
1974, '75, '78, '79

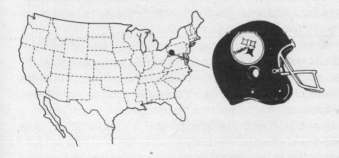

For almost forty years the Steelers were just any other team.
In the seventies, they were *the* team, possibly the most
powerful unit the game has ever known. Four Super Bowl
victories in the space of six years reflects the Steelers'
domination, and this wonderful era rightly overshadows the
early struggles endured by the club.

Football came to the steel city in 1933 when a former
boxer, Art Rooney, bought the franchise and named his
team the Pirates. In their first two seasons the Pirates
finished bottom of their division and, before Rooney
changed the name to the Steelers in 1940, the team had a
record of twenty-four wins to sixty-two defeats.

It was 1942 before the Steelers had their first winning
season (seven victories to four defeats), and after the war

and a largely unsuccessful merger with the Philadelphia Eagles, more problems hit the club.

In 1947, just before a play-off game with Philadelphia, the players went on a one-day strike in support of a pay claim. Not surprisingly, the stricken Steelers were beaten 21–0.

Head coaches came and went and the team rarely looked like winning honours until 1969, when Rooney appointed the fourteenth coach in the club's 36-year history. Chuck Noll had been assistant coach to the successful Baltimore Colts, and his arrival at Pittsburgh proved to be the turning point for the Steelers.

Noll set about rebuilding the team, largely with college players. He began his recruiting with a formidable defensive tackle called 'Mean' Joe Greene, and in 1970 – when the Steelers were one of three NFL teams to be transferred to the AFL on the merger of the leagues – Noll added a quarterback, Terry Bradshaw, who was one of the best prospects around.

Greene was the central figure in a defensive line known as the 'Steel Curtain', and Bradshaw led the attack with a real killer instinct.

Noll's construction of the team was virtually completed by the signing of running back Franco Harris in 1972 when the Steelers had their best season so far, winning the Central Division for the first time. The Steelers were beaten by the Miami Dolphins in the conference championship game but they were about to become the team everyone else had to beat.

The Steelers had only to wait until 1974 before they took the conference title. After finishing on top of their division (a feat they repeated for the following five seasons) they beat the Oakland Raiders to win the conference and then went on to defeat the Minnesota Vikings in the Super

Bowl, Harris claiming a Super Bowl rushing record in the process.

The Steelers repeated their triumph the next season by beating the Dallas Cowboys 21–17. Bradshaw had his best-ever season in 1978, when the unstoppable Steelers added a third Super Bowl with a repeat victory over Dallas. And to underline their claim to be the team of the decade, the Steelers returned to the Super Bowl in 1979, beating the Los Angeles Rams 31–19 to become the first club to win four Super Bowls.

Although the Steelers continued to win their division into the eighties, the retirement of Bradshaw and Harris in 1983 signalled the end of an era, and in 1985 they suffered their first losing season since 1971.

ST LOUIS CARDINALS

National Conference, East Division
Stadium: Busch Stadium, St Louis
Capacity: 51,392   **Surface:** Artificial
Colours: Cardinal red, black and white
Championships: Division, 1974, '75; NFL, 1925, '47

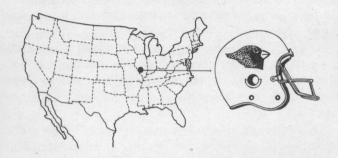

The Cardinals go back to the very roots of the game itself, and, although they have undergone several changes of name and location, they have valid reason to consider themselves the oldest surviving club in the game.

It was 1898 when a football team from the poor district of Chicago (known as the Chicago Normals) bought a set of faded maroon jerseys from the city's university team. When taunted about their cast-off strip, the club's founder, decorator Chris O'Brien, said proudly, 'That's not maroon, it's cardinal red'. Immediately the team was re-christened the Racine (the name of their ground) Cardinals.

The team was disbanded twice because of lack of competition and the First World War but the Racine Cardinals survived to become founder members of the American Professional Football League on its inception in 1920.

The NFL Clubs

In 1922 they changed their name to the Chicago Cardinals and moved to Whitesox Park to share the ground of the city's baseball team. By that time the league had become the NFL, and in 1925, with twenty teams in operation, the Cardinals took their first championship, winning eleven of their fourteen games.

This was to prove the Cardinals' only taste of glory for some years, and, beginning in 1933, they finished bottom of their division six times in eight seasons. Ownership fell to Chicago business magnate Charles Bidwell, and he injected a lot of his own money into the club, signing players on big contracts. However, he never saw the fruit of his investment. He died in 1947 just before the Cardinals beat the Philadelphia Eagles for their second NFL championship.

The following season they returned to contest the NFL championship game but were beaten on this occasion by the Eagles. With off-the-field rows affecting the team's performances, the fifties were highlighted only by a spectacular 53–14 victory over their deadly enemies, the Chicago Bears, in 1955.

In 1960, with NFL–AFL rivalry at its peak, the NFL transferred the Cardinals to St Louis in an attempt to prevent the AFL from establishing a team there. The Cardinals' start in their new home could hardly have been better; they beat the Los Angeles Rams 43–21 in the first game.

However, problems again loomed in the background. In 1964 there were rumours that the Cardinals were to move to Atlanta because the building of their new stadium was so much behind schedule. But they resisted the move and in 1966 took belated occupation of the magnificent Busch Stadium.

In 1974 and 1975 the Cardinals won their division but failed to make any impression in the play-offs. And by 1985, uncertainty for the future returned, with talk of the club moving to Phoenix, Arizona.

SAN DIEGO CHARGERS

American Conference, West Division
Stadium: Jack Murphy Stadium, San Diego
Capacity: 60,100   **Surface:** Grass
Colours: Blue, gold and white
Championships: Division, 1979, '80, '81; AFL, 1963

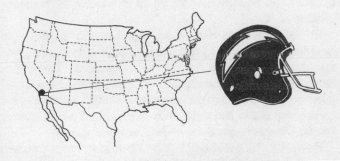

The Chargers began life in Los Angeles in 1960 as one of the original franchises of the AFL. They played their opening game at the Los Angeles Coliseum (now the home of the Raiders) but their impressive victory over the New York Titans was watched by only a tiny crowd.

Throughout that first season, which ended with the Chargers winning their division, attendances were very poor, and the club's owner, Barron Hilton (president of the Hilton Hotel chain), announced a loss of $1 million. The following season, Hilton was given permission to move the club to San Diego, where there was felt to be more of a demand for a football team.

The ploy worked, crowds began to show a steady increase, and, for the second season in succession, the Chargers gave their fans something to shout about by winning their divisional title. The Chargers continued their monopoly of the division throughout the early days of the AFL – only twice in the first seven years did the title fail to go to San Diego.

The Chargers' best season was 1963, when they established a reputation for attacking play that still stands today. They lost only three of their fourteen matches and went on to crush the Boston Patriots 51–10 to win the AFL championship.

In 1967 the club moved to their present home – the beautifully appointed Jack Murphy Stadium, named after the sports editor of a San Diego newspaper. Two years later, every seat in the stadium was taken when the Chargers' biggest crowd in their history – 54,000 – was attracted by the visit of Joe Namath's New York Jets. A 34–27 victory for the Chargers gave the club a further impetus.

However, this great day failed to herald a prosperous era for the club. Sid Gillman, who had been head coach since the Chargers' very first game, retired in 1969, returned in 1970 and then retired for good in 1971. This did little for the club's morale, and in 1970 and 1971 they had losing seasons.

Desperate measures were needed, and the signing of veteran quarterback Johnny Unitas from the Baltimore Colts was certainly an act of desperation. Unitas, one of the all-time greats, was 40 years of age, and after only three games the return of an old back injury put him out of action for ever.

A rookie, Dan Fouts, took over as quarterback and he gradually steered the Chargers back to respectability, overcoming their worst-ever season in 1975 when they managed to win only two games. In 1978 the Chargers had their best campaign for nine years and the following season became West Division champions. The Chargers went on to complete a hat-trick of divisional titles, and in 1985 their offense gained a season's total of 6,535 yards, the third highest aggregate in the 66-year history of the NFL.

SAN FRANCISCO 49ers

National Conference, West Division
Stadium: Candlestick Park, San Francisco
Capacity: 61,413 **Surface:** Grass
Colours: Gold and scarlet
Championships: Division, 1970, '71, '72, '81, '83, '84, '86;
Conference, 1981, '84; Super Bowl, 1981, '84

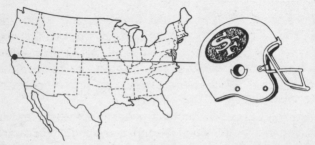

The 49ers – their name a reference to the gold rush of 1849 which brought prospectors flocking to California – were members of the rebel All American Football Conference in 1946 and, when that league disbanded, were accepted into the NFL in 1950.

But their entry into the major league was by no means a successful one, as the 49ers won only three games all season. Their climb to the top was to be a slow one, but they were quick to earn a reputation for inventive offense tactics.

In 1957 the 49ers brought into the game a pass play that became known as the 'Alley Oop' pass, whereby the ball was thrown on a very high, looping arc and was caught by the 6ft 5in R. C. Owens, who was able to out-jump the opposition. They also invented, in 1960, an attacking formation called the 'shotgun', for which the quarterback, instead of standing just behind the line of scrimmage, stands up to 5 yards behind it, giving himself more time to decide what to do with the ball when it is released to him. It is a risky ploy, but with it the 49ers won four of their last five games of the season.

Yet even with these novel ideas, the 49ers failed to make a significant impression and, losing faith in the 'shotgun' formation, they had their worst season ever in 1963, winning only two games.

It was not until 1970 that the 49ers claimed a title, and their triumph in the NFC West Division was one that was repeated for the following two seasons, but each time they lost to the Dallas Cowboys in the play-offs. In the middle of this run, in 1971, the 49ers moved to a new home at Candlestick Park.

Perhaps the most important event in the 49ers' recent history came in 1977 when the club was bought by Edward De Bartolo Jr who, at 31, became the youngest owner in football and had bright ideas to match his youth.

After a dreadful season in 1978 – two wins, fourteen defeats – De Bartolo appointed the well-respected college coach Bill Walsh as head coach of the 49ers. Under Walsh, the 49ers emerged from a bleak period of eight losing seasons in nine and five changes of head coach.

By 1981 he had built a team to win the Super Bowl, losing only three matches all season and taking the crown with victory over the Cincinnati Bengals. The full measure of Walsh's achievement is seen in the fact that, in three seasons, he had taken the club from the worst record in the NFL to the best record.

More was to come in 1984 when the 49ers lost only one of their sixteen regular season games, winning every away match. They went on to establish more landmarks by beating the Miami Dolphins 38–16 in Super Bowl XIX, breaking twelve Super Bowl records and equalling four others.

SEATTLE SEAHAWKS

American Conference, West Division
Stadium: Kingdome, Seattle
Capacity: 69,984   **Surface:** Artificial
Colours: Blue, green and silver
Championships: None

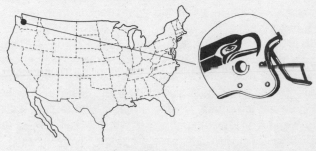

It was not until 1976 that the Seahawks played their first game in the NFL, but the story of professional football in Seattle began four years earlier. In 1972 a group of prominent Seattle businessmen and community figures formed a company with the intention of bidding for an NFL franchise.

They began working on the construction of the Kingdome, a space-age stadium that was to cost $7 million. It would house 65,000 spectators and would have the world's largest self-supporting concrete roof.

The investment paid off in 1974 when the NFL, in an effort to expand the game, granted a franchise to Seattle, which was to become the north-western outpost for the sport.

Interest in the new club was phenomenal, and more than 20,000 entries were received in the contest to give the team a name. By a massive majority, Seahawks was adopted. As the build-up to the Seahawks' initial game intensified, so did the locals' interest, and even today Seattle supporters are acknowledged to be among the most fanatical in the game.

Before a ball was kicked in the Kingdome, season-ticket sales touched 60,000 and had to stop. Given such over-whelming support, it was a disappointment that their first season in 1976 was largely unsuccessful, with only two victories. However, their 1977 record – five wins, nine defeats – was the best second-year record of any team in NFL history.

By 1978 it was as if the Seahawks were a long-established fixture, and, in winning nine of their sixteen games, they showed just how far they had come in such a short time. Their offense could hold its own with any in the league, but the defense revealed signs of cracking under pressure. This was to be dramatically illustrated in 1980 when the Seahawks conceded a massive 408 points (the worst record in the league) and finished with only four wins.

The Seahawks looked to former Buffalo Bills and LA Rams coach Chuck Knox to build a solid defense, and in his first season he took the club to the play-offs as a wild-card qualifier, only for the LA Raiders to snuff out their chances. The Seahawks were only spurred on to greater efforts by this setback and had their best-ever season in 1984, win-ning twelve games but losing to the Miami Dolphins in the play-offs.

TAMPA BAY BUCCANEERS

National Conference, Central Division
Stadium: Tampa Stadium, Florida
Capacity: 74,315   **Surface:** Grass
Colours: Orange, white and red
Championships: Division, 1979, '81

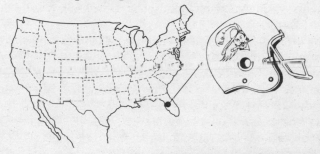

Like Seattle, the Buccaneers joined in 1976 under the NFL's expansion policy, but football had been played in Tampa Bay as early as 1968, when the Washington Redskins met the Atlanta Falcons in a pre-season game.

Other, mainly successful, pre-season matches were held at Tampa Stadium, and this is what prompted the NFL, in 1974, to announce that the franchise was being granted to property investor Hugh Culverhouse for $16 million.

The Buccaneers was adopted as the club's name with a swashbuckling emblem on the helmet to match. However, there was nothing dashing about the club's entry into the NFL in 1976. In their first season, the Buccaneers made history by becoming the first club to lose all their fourteen regular season games, including five matches in which they failed to score a point.

The nightmare continued into the following season, with twelve straight losses at the start of the campaign. And then, on 11 December 1977, the Buccaneers at last won a game, beating the New Orleans Saints 33–14 – and away from home at that!

A week later they made it two in a row with the defeat of St Louis, and at least the season ended on a relatively high note.

The arrival of quarterback Doug Williams in 1978 helped the Buccaneers to maintain their progress, and they finished the season with five wins. This improvement was the boost that was needed by the club, and in 1979 the team that had been written off as no-hopers won their division, made it to the play-offs and were beaten only 9–0 by the LA Rams in the conference championship game.

No longer could they be regarded as a joke outfit, and to emphasize this they were back in the play-offs in 1981. However, a 38–0 defeat by the powerful Dallas Cowboys was a disaster the Buccaneers took a long time to forget.

Apart from the strike-hit 1982 season, the club have not had a winning campaign since that terrible afternoon against the Cowboys. Indeed, in 1985, they were back to their bad old ways, winning twice, losing fourteen times and scoring a meagre 125 points all year, joint worst in the NFL.

The NFL Clubs

WASHINGTON REDSKINS

National Conference, East Division
Stadium: Robert F. Kennedy Stadium, Washington
Capacity: 55,431   **Surface:** Grass
Colours: Burgundy and gold
Championships: Division, 1972, '83, '84; Conference, 1972, '82, '83; Super Bowl, 1982; NFL, 1937, '42

The Redskins moved to Washington in 1937 and immediately rewarded their new fans by winning the NFL championship. Prior to that, the club had been operating in Boston, where it was founded in 1932 as the Boston Braves.

In 1933 they shared the ground of the Boston Red Sox baseball team and changed their name to the Redskins. They appointed as coach a full-blooded Red Indian – Will 'Lone Star' Dietz – and for the official photograph on the team's first practice day, the players all wore Red Indian head-dresses and warpaint.

Such gimmicks, however, failed to help the club stave off financial problems which forced on them the move to Washington. Always with his eye on publicity and showmanship, the club's owner, George Marshall, pioneered a tradition (still very much part of the game today) of spectacular half-time shows, marching bands and cheerleaders.

Marshall also brought the great quarterback, Sammy Baugh, to the club, and it was he who led the Redskins to the championship in 1937 and again in 1942 when they beat the Chicago Bears.

Baugh retired in 1952, but by that time the team were already showing signs of decline, and Marshall came under severe attack, particularly for his failure to recruit any black players. In fact, it was 1962 before a black player joined the Redskins.

The sixties produced only disappointment for the club, but the good times were to return in 1969 when the legendary coach Vince Lombardi joined in an advisory role. Under his direction the Redskins enjoyed their first winning season since 1955. Sadly, just two weeks before the start of the following season, Lombardi died of cancer.

The foundations Lombardi had laid were built on by his successor, George Allen, and the 1972 season saw the Redskins make it to the Super Bowl, where they lost to the Miami Dolphins.

In Allen's seven-year spell with the Redskins, they reached the play-offs five times, and when he turned his back on Washington in 1979 he left them with a side of great potential and an explosive quarterback, Joe Theismann.

Theismann inspired the team in 1978 to their best-ever start to a season – six victories in a row – before going on, in 1982, to avenge the Super Bowl defeat by Miami.

The Redskins had to wait ten years, but revenge was sweet when, with running back John Riggins in magnificent form, they beat the Dolphins 27–17 in Super Bowl XVII. The Redskins looked set to equal the achievements of Green Bay, Miami and Pittsburgh by winning two consecutive Super Bowls but were crushed by the LA Raiders the following year.

8 THE HALL OF FAME AND GREATS OF AMERICAN FOOTBALL

EVEN THOUGH American football is a relatively young sport and has existed as a professional game only for sixty-seven years, it has had a history rich in incident and personalities. And it is entirely appropriate that the past should be treasured and celebrated in a shrine dedicated to the game.

The Pro Football Hall of Fame stands on the outskirts of Canton, Ohio – the birthplace of the professional code – and is dedicated to the game's heroes, portraying in lavish exhibition halls the men and the events which have shaped the sport.

The Hall of Fame opened its doors in September 1963 and, by the summer of 1985, 4 million people had passed through it. By then it had more than doubled in size into a four-building complex – the centrepiece of which was a circular exhibition centre whose roof was football-shaped – with more than 51,000 square feet of display space.

The Hall of Fame is brimful of NFL memorabilia, with 15,000 photographs, 7,500 programmes, 2,500 books, 500 miles of film and a collection of paintings. They tell the story of American football, from its humble beginnings as a professional sport in a car showroom near the Hall of Fame, to the present-day game, the passion of a nation.

But the Hall of Fame is more than just a collection of memories. It also honours the achievements of the best professional players. To be elected into the Hall of Fame is the ambition of every player who takes the field in the NFL and, for many, this honour outstrips any medals or records.

Every year, new members are elected to the Hall of Fame by a board of twenty-nine selectors comprising football writers from each city that houses an NFL team, plus the president of the Pro Football Writers' Association. Between four and seven are elected each year – they have to be nominated and then draw a minimum 80 per cent support from the panel of selectors.

Anyone can nominate a person to be considered for the Hall of Fame, but the conditions are that players must have retired for at least five years before they are eligible, coaches may have just retired to be considered, while administrators or owners can be elected at any time.

When the Hall of Fame opened in 1963, seventeen 'charter' members were elected, going right back to the first years of the pro game, including figures such as Jim Thorpe, Red Grange and George Halas.

By 1986, the total number elected was 133, and each one has his own place in the 'enshrinement halls'. The Hall of Fame will continue to grow each year and, with every new enshrinee, the pressure on space in the buildings becomes greater. Who knows how much the Hall of Fame will expand in future years?

I have selected five figures – four who have already been inducted into the Hall of Fame, and one who is certain to be in future years. They represent different eras and different elements of the game, but collectively, they stand for everything that is good in the sport . . .

JIM BROWN
Running back, Cleveland Browns 1957–65

In nine seasons with Cleveland, Jim Brown never missed one game through injury, and he established a host of records that remained unchallenged for more than twenty years. At 6ft 2ins and 16½ stones, he was a massive figure in every sense, and there are many who believe that he is the greatest running back the game has ever seen.

JIM BROWN

The statistics certainly back up this claim. When he retired from the game to pursue a career in films in 1965, he had gained a total of 12,312 yards – no player had previously broken the 10,000-yard barrier. He averaged 104 yards per game, a phenomenal record when it is considered that gaining 100 yards in a match is a task roughly equivalent to scoring a century in cricket.

He joined the Browns from Syracuse University, where he had already built up a formidable reputation, both as a footballer and as a baseball player. Indeed, he was offered a place in the New York Yankees baseball team before settling on football, and in his fourth game in the NFL, he showed that he had made the correct decision. Against the Los Angeles Rams, Brown was virtually unstoppable, running for 237 yards, a record for one game. He went on to run for more than 200 yards on three later occasions but never beat this total.

Brown, who had the power to resist the most physical of challenges and the ability to surge through the smallest gap, would often leave a trail of would-be tacklers in his wake on his way to a touchdown. He scored 126 touchdowns in his career, which remains the highest individual total in the game's history.

He was clearly the focal point of the Cleveland attack, but even though opposing teams concentrated their efforts on stopping Brown, he always semed to find a way through and, with his inspiration, the Browns won the NFL Championship in 1964.

Brown was 29 years old when he opted for Hollywood (he has appeared in several well-known films) and there is little doubt that he still had a few good years in the no. 32 jersey left in him. He might well have further secured his place in history by setting targets that could never be beaten. As it is, only one man, Walter Payton of the Chicago Bears, has surpassed Brown's total yardage.

GEORGE HALAS
Offensive end, coach, owner, Chicago Bears 1920–1983

In sixty years in the game, George Halas was quite simply the most influential figure in American football. Known as 'Papa Bear', he was more than just the man who started the Chicago Bears, he was one of the founding fathers of professional football, and in his time as a player, coach, owner and administrator, he was constantly looking for ways to develop the game.

The Hall of Fame and Greats of American Football

Halas was one of the leading characters in the meeting in 1920 which led to the establishment of a professional league. At that time he was running the works team of A. E. Staley Starch Manufacturers in Decatur, a town near Chicago. His team, called the Decatur Staleys, were the forerunners of the Chicago Bears; by 1921, they had moved to Chicago, and by 1922 they had adopted the name Bears and were now under the ownership of Halas, who was also player–coach.

GEORGE HALAS

He was never one of the game's great players, but he was no mean blocker and played as offensive end for eleven years. He weighed only a shade over 13 stone but made up for his comparative lack of bulk with his skill and cunning. But it was as a coach that he made the most of these attributes, and some of his innovations changed the way the game was played.

Halas was primarily responsible for introducing the attacking line-up known as the 'T' formation, which most teams still adopt at the line of scrimmage. The players would line up in the shape of a 'T', with the linemen forming the top of the 'T' and the quarterback and the three running backs forming the upright and bottom of the 'T' (see p.27).

With this formation, the Bears won the 1940 Championship, defeating the Washington Redskins 73–0, a record score that is unlikely ever to be beaten. Halas coached the Bears for a total of forty years – split into four periods of ten years each – and, of the 506 games in which he was in charge, the Bears won 326, another mark that will stand in the record books for a long time.

Between 1921 and 1963 the Bears won the NFL Championship on six occasions, and when, after a long period of limited success, they won the 1986 Super Bowl – two years after Halas had died at the age of 88 – they dedicated the victory to his memory. Engraved on the rings that were presented to each member of the victorious Bears are the initials: GSH.

The Bears are, and probably always will be, the team of George Halas, and his family influence still lives on. The club president, Michael McCaskey, is Halas's grandson, and several other blood relatives occupy high-ranking positions in the Bears' organization.

VINCE LOMBARDI
Coach, Green Bay Packers, 1959–67; Washington Redskins, 1969

The man who gave his name to the trophy awarded to the Super Bowl victors, coach Lombardi was the brains behind one of the greatest teams in the history of American football, the Green Bay Packers of the mid-sixties.

Lombardi, who had learned his trade as assistant coach with the New York Giants, joined the Packers in 1959 at the age of 45 and, in nine seasons at Green Bay, he led them to five championships, including victory in the first two

Super Bowls (hence the dedication to him of the silver trophy).

Lombardi's success can be seen in its true light when placed against the fact that, when he took over as head coach of the Packers, the club had just suffered a miserable season during which they had won only one of their eleven games.

VINCE LOMBARDI

Lombardi's unique methods of getting the most from players, by inspiring fear and loyalty in equal amounts, soon saw the Packers on the upturn, and in his first season he led them to seven victories, their best record for fifteen years. One of the Green Bay players said of Lombardi: 'We all knew that he bled inside for us, he just loved us,' while another said of his approach: 'Lombardi's very fair. He treats us all like dogs.'

Either way, Lombardi – in a relatively brief time – became something of a legend, and is probably the most quoted coach of all time. He is credited with possibly the game's most famous saying – 'Winning isn't everything, it is the *only* thing' – and certainly it was his methods of motivating his players, rather than any fancy ploys on the field, that earned Lombardi his reputation and his record.

After doing all he could at Green Bay, Lombardi

accepted an offer to become part-owner and head coach of the Washington Redskins, who were then in just as dreadful a state as the Packers had been when he arrived on the scene some ten years earlier.

In his first season at Washington, he reversed the decline and looked set to prove that his achievements at Green Bay had been no accident. Yet as the Redskins were preparing for the 1970 season, eager to continue their revival, Lombardi died of cancer. He was 57.

A man of the magnitude of Lombardi cannot be summed up by mere statistics, yet the record of his coaching career does reflect his greatness. He never endured a losing season and, in 146 games, his team won on 105 occasions – a percentage of victories that is unlikely to be equalled.

JOE NAMATH
Quarterback, New York Jets 1965–76; Los Angeles Rams 1977

Namath was the game's first media superstar, his reputation on the field matched by an ability to be in the news when he wasn't playing. Known as 'Broadway Joe' – a reference to New York's street of theatres and stars – Namath attracted publicity wherever he went, usually holding hands with a famous film actress.

For a decade, Namath was the game's most glamorous figure, but his off-the-field activities would not have attracted so much attention were it not for the fact that, when he wore the green jersey of the Jets, he threw the ball as well as, if not better than, anyone had ever done. In three of his first four seasons, Namath passed for a total of 3,000 yards – a remarkable tally. And in 1967, he became the first player to pass the ball more than 4,000 yards in a season.

His unswerving accuracy, and his refusal to be ruffled under the most intense pressure, gave the Jets an enormous advantage over their rivals and, while they had players in other positions who could hold their own with the best, they were known as Namath's team while he was in charge.

JOE NAMATH

Namath first became a national figure when, as the AFL's representatives in Super Bowl III, the Jets met the mighty Baltimore Colts, and he announced at a function: 'I guarantee we will win the Super Bowl'. Such boasting from the underdogs – no AFL team had yet won the Super Bowl – was predicted to rebound on Namath, but instead he led the Jets to a shock 16–7 victory. Although he did not throw one touchdown pass, Namath was voted the game's Most Valuable Player, and a legend was born.

Namath joined the Jets as a rookie in 1965 from Alabama University, and, as a much-prized talent at a time when the AFL–NFL war was at its most intense, his decision to take the vast sum of money on offer at New York quickly made him a noteworthy character. His early performances quickly repaid the faith and money invested in him, and his charisma and playboy appeal ensured that the Jets always played to packed stadiums. By 1972, Namath was the game's highest paid player, but soon natural decay began to take its toll.

A series of knee injuries, which neither operations nor the wearing of braces could mend, kept him out of the game for long periods and, never able to rediscover his momentum, his explosive talent rather fizzled out. Still with knee problems, he decided to try his luck on the west coast with the Los Angeles Rams in 1977. But he played only six times for the Rams, retiring after a disastrous game, which had been televised coast-to-coast.

Namath, American football's first superstar in the modern sense of the word, is still very much in demand as a commentator and pundit, and although his playing career ended in disaster, there are many who believe he was the greatest passer of a ball the game has ever known. He was inducted into the Hall of Fame in 1985.

WALTER PAYTON
Running back, Chicago Bears 1975–

On 7 October 1984, in a relatively unimportant match between the Chicago Bears and the New Orleans Saints, a major slice of American football history was made. Walter Payton became, statistically at least, the game's greatest all-time running back. His 154 yards in the Bears' victory over the Saints took him past Jim Brown's career mark of 12,312, and Payton, who has now played for the Bears for twelve seasons, has gone on, week by week, to stretch his lead at the head of the all-time list. He has now rushed for almost 4,000 more yards than Brown.

The Hall of Fame and Greats of American Football

The fact that Payton – a marvellous athlete at 5ft 11in and 14½ stone – has filled this most demanding role for the Bears for so·many seasons, and with very few injuries, testifies to his durability and strength, assets which are as prized in a running back as the ability to burst through the narrowest of gaps.

WALTER PAYTON

The Bears' coach, Mike Ditka, is not given to overstatement so his tribute to Payton – 'He's the best football player I've ever seen. At any position, he's a complete player' – can be seen as a realistic appraisal of his attributes. Similarly, that Payton was able to amass his series of records while playing for a Bears team that, until 1985, was largely unsuccessful, further stresses his greatness.

Consistency and dependability are the qualities which characterize Payton, whose soft-spoken, relaxed attitude have made him a favourite off the field as well. It is remarkable that, in breaking the all-time rushing record, Payton only once headed the season's table of leading rushers. That was in 1977 when he notched up 1,852 yards, almost 600 yards ahead of his nearest rival.

In his time, Payton has taken twenty-one club records and five NFL records – including the highest single-game rushing tally of 275 yards – but it is his dedication to hard work that has won him most admirers. Even though he is one of the biggest stars in the game today, Payton never relaxes his formidable schedule of training, completing gruelling sessions in and out of season which help to make him one of the fittest, strongest men on the Bears' roster.

He can run 40 yards in 4.5 seconds and has the physique to withstand the terrifying tackles he has to face in one of the most exposed positions in the game.

At 32, it is difficult to imagine Payton playing for too many more seasons but, while he maintains his fitness, there is no reason why he should not go on to set career rushing records that will *never* be beaten. As a player who is still in active service, Payton is not yet eligible to be inducted into the Hall of Fame but there is no doubt that, at the earliest possible opportunity, his name will join the others in the game's pantheon.

9 THE COLLEGE GAME

AMERICAN FOOTBALL began in the colleges of the United States in the late 1800s, and for today's professional players it still begins there. The journey to a place in an NFL team commences at college, where promising players learn the game before graduating to the professional ranks.

In fact, many budding players learn little else in their time at college. They are awarded football scholarships, and academic pursuits play very little part in their timetable. The colleges can afford this because their football teams, as well as bringing prestige and possible glory, are big business, for although college football is often seen as little more than a nursery for the NFL, there is a huge spectator interest in it as well.

There is no college equivalent of the Super Bowl, as the game is split into regional conferences and there is no national championship, but the four biggest games of the season – the Rose Bowl, the Orange Bowl, the Sugar Bowl and the Cotton Bowl – draw crowds as huge as those of the Super Bowl. In 1985, more than 25 million spectators attended top level college football, which gives some clue to its popularity.

The standard of football is high and, although the college players are strictly amateur, the game is run on very professional lines, and the star performers are well looked after. A successful team brings more than honour to a college – when the University Colleges of Los Angeles and Iowa met in the 1985 Rose Bowl, they shared receipts of more than $4 million.

To recruit promising players to their college, the bigger establishments have a large scouting network with which they hope to discover future talent at high schools. Each scout has an area to cover and contacts every high school in that area for details on youngsters with potential. By means of weekly questionnaires, relating mainly to attitude and ambition, the scout and the college's coaches will decide whether a player has got what it takes. They will have already assessed his physical attributes and, if he meets their requirements, he will be offered a football scholarship.

Once at college, the budding footballer is given an education in the game second to none. He is taught by a highly paid team of coaches and has as much time as he wants to perfect his technique and build up his physique.

The coaching staff at a top college is just as impressive as that of many NFL clubs, with the money the colleges earn from attendances, private sponsors and television deals going towards providing lucrative contracts for top coaches.

However, even though there is a huge amount of interest and money in the college game, it is nevertheless the number two attraction beside the professional league. Such was not always the case and, long after the NFL was established in 1921, college football still held sway as far as public popularity was concerned.

While huge crowds turned up to watch the students well into the 1930s, the professional game attracted paltry attendances and was sneered at by most football fans. Yet until the NFL was born, there was nowhere for the college players to continue playing after they had finished as students and, by the mid-1930s, it became a natural progression that, once finished at college, the players would join the professionals.

Soon the public seized the opportunity to carry on watching the players who had starred for the colleges, and attendances for NFL games soared. In 1936, in order to regulate the competition for college players, the NFL instituted the draft system. This was to combat the effect of the richer, more powerful clubs always being able to attract the best new players, while the poor got poorer.

The draft system was brought in to even things out. It meant that, at the end of each season, the team which finished with the poorest record in the NFL would have the first choice when the college players were drafted for the following season. The second worst team would have the second choice, and so on down the league.

This invariably ensured that the most highly regarded college player would be signed on by the worst professional club, thereby giving a struggling club a massive boost – both in terms of playing strength and also because the biggest star in the colleges would undoubtedly be a crowd-puller. It also meant that the poorer teams would, over a few years, build a stronger playing staff by having one of the first draft choices.

The system, brought in fifty years ago, has stood the test of time. Every spring, the NFL clubs take their chance to draft the pick of the colleges' talent in rotation, the twenty-eighth most successful club having the first pick, the Super Bowl winners having the twenty-eighth pick. The pecking order remains the same over twelve rounds of selections.

The most coveted college player is usually the winner of the Heisman Trophy, awarded annually to the player who, in the opinion of a panel of judges, is the best in the game. The trophy is named after John H. Heisman, a great coach at the turn of the century and the man who first brought the forward pass into American football.

A panel of sports writers also decides which college team is the strongest each year. There is no end-of-season tournament to decide the rankings, but, in each area, they have their own championship match, or Bowl, to settle the local supremacy.

The top colleges are split up into ten regional conferences, with each having a title decider between the two most successful teams over the course of the season. The oldest such championship game is the Rose Bowl, held in California since 1902, and together with the Orange Bowl (held in Miami), the Sugar Bowl (New Orleans) and the Cotton Bowl (Dallas) it represents one of the Big Four college football games.

As well as the colleges which belong to the conferences, there are a large number of independent colleges who, instead of a regular fixture list involving the same teams, prefer to take on any college from any area. Among the independent colleges is one of the best all-time teams, Notre Dame, who have been voted national champions more times than any other college.

☆ 10 THE GAME OUTSIDE AMERICA ☆

THERE IS a tendency to regard the existence of American football in Britain as a recent phenomenon, yet while there has been a huge upsurge in interest in the sport since Channel 4 first screened its weekly highlights programme in 1982, the earliest recorded match on these shores took place as long ago as 1910.

It was then that two teams composed of American naval recruits played an exhibition match in Kent in front of a sizeable and curious crowd of around 4,000. While the event was a success, it did not spark much interest in playing the game among Britons, and the action was restricted to American exiles who, particularly after the Second World War, played games among themselves. The game might well have continued to lie dormant – played only by American Air Force men stationed in Britain – had it not been for Channel 4's decision to give a weekly slot to a programme of highlights from the previous weekend's NFL matches.

Immediately, an army of armchair fans was discovered, and for millions of Britons, American football represented the thrills and excitement that had gone from some of our more traditional sports. Channel 4, who had thought they were catering for a minority interest, were amazed by the viewer response. The show was hosted by Nicky Horne, a disc jockey who knew nothing about the game and joined the audience in the learning process. He was partnered by a former NFL player, and could ask all the elementary questions everyone who was watching wanted to ask.

This presentation, combined with the expert packaging of highlights, provided an attractive blend to a public who had become gradually disenchanted with our version of football. By 1985, the weekly audience had risen to four million and, since 1983, the Super Bowl has been televised live in Britain. Although it continued well into the early hours of the morning, Super Bowl XXI was watched at one point by 3½ million people.

The interest and expertise among the viewing public was such that, for the start of the 1986 season, Nicky Horne was replaced by Frank Gifford, a former player in the NFL and now a well-known and experienced commentator, and the weekly programme was broadcast from America. No longer could American football be treated as an obscure sport, followed only by a minority of devotees.

Naturally, the interest in the game did not simply begin and end with watching it on television. As soon as it hit British screens, teams started up, and by 1986 there were some 120 teams regularly playing in Britain, with a total of 6,000 players involved in the game.

The first team to be formed were the London Ravens, who are the country's strongest side and who have blossomed from their early days practising in Hyde Park to end the 1986 season undefeated. The Ravens took part in the first official British league game, against the Manchester Spartans in the summer of 1983.

As the game in Britain mushroomed, so problems of organization materialized. The Ravens and the Spartans, together with teams from Milton Keynes, Poole and North-ampton, began playing each other on a haphazard, but semi-organized, basis and by 1985 had established their own league, called the American Football League. Most of the big clubs joined this league, but a rival set-up, the British American Football Federation, came into being at the same time and also contained some useful teams.

The BAFF, with twelve teams, was very much the junior partner; the AFL had the higher standards (even though the teams were still of very poor quality compared to those in America) and at the end of their first season in 1985, a crowd of more than 7,000 was attracted to the AFL's first championship game, called the Summer Bowl. The London Ravens were the league's inaugural champions, beating the Streatham Olympians 45–7.

At the end of a satisfactory 1985 season for both leagues, the talk of a merger became a reality, and the rival orga-nizations amalgamated to form the British American Foot-ball League. But a year later the British game was in chaos again. Budweiser, the American brewing company who wanted to tie themselves to the growth of the game in Britain, sank sponsorship money of £250,000 into the crea-tion of a new league, called the Budweiser League.

Attracted by the prospect of a well-organized, financially secure and sponsored league, most clubs deserted the BAFL to join the new league. The clubs who left the BAFL included all their top names, particularly the London Ravens and the other five clubs who had taken part in the previous season's play-offs.

Again the game's development was fragmented, with eighty teams in the Budweiser League and forty remaining in the BAFL. The Ravens and the Olympians met again in the first Budweiser Bowl in 1986, and once more the Ravens triumphed. But the crowd was only 6,000 and, for the BAFL's Summer Bowl, in which the Birmingham Bulls defeated the Glasgow Lions, the attendance was even smaller. It became obvious that unless a nationally-organized league, involving all the country's top teams, could be set up, the game stood the chance of facing a decline in standards and interest.

Wisely, the rift between the Budweiser League and the BAFL was patched up in time for the 1987 season to start – the British season runs from April to September – and a unified league was established under the umbrella of the Budweiser organization.

The BAFL clubs were merged into the Budweiser League, comprising a national league involving 105 clubs on three levels. The three-tier structure of the new league is thus: a National Division, which is split into four regional conferences and which contains the strongest teams; a Premier Division, split into six regional conferences and which involves clubs of a lesser standard than the National Division; and Division One, which comprises the rest of the clubs, divided into eight conferences. The winners of the four regional conferences of the National Division compete in the play-offs to decide the Budweiser League champions.

It is to be hoped that, with this well-designed structure, the game in Britain can overcome its early birth pains and go on to gain in strength. Standards of the British clubs will continue to trail those in America – the Brighton B52s won all but one of their domestic games in 1986 and then went to America and were beaten 76–0 by a San Francisco college team – but in the long-term future it is conceivable that a team of British-born players could compete on equal terms with their American cousins.

The Game Outside America

There is persistent talk that the next time the NFL decides to expand by granting a franchise to another club, it might opt to come to London and increase the boundaries of the professional game to include Europe. If this were the case – and as yet it is only a rumour – it would clearly have to be a team composed of experienced NFL-quality players.

What has encouraged talk of such a move has been the remarkable success of one-off games staged in London. In 1983, when interest in the sport had just begun to grow, the St Louis Cardinals and the Minnesota Vikings played an exhibition game at Wembley Stadium and drew more than 30,000.

Three years later, in August 1986, the then Super Bowl champions, the Chicago Bears, played the Dallas Cowboys as part of their pre-season preparations. This time the crowd at Wembley was an all-ticket one of 86,000, and for weeks before the game tickets were almost as difficult to come by as ones for the FA Cup Final. Despite the dreadful weather – it rained incessantly throughout the game – and the fact that both teams were giving a run-out to most of their unknown youngsters, it was adjudged a great success by the fans, many of whom had stood up for four hours or more, and by the travelling NFL officials.

There is every likelihood that a pre-season exhibition game at Wembley Stadium will become an annual event on the NFL calendar. For the British followers, who are clearly captivated by the pageantry and glamour of the live game, it is likely to be a well-supported fixture.

The growth of the game away from the shores of America is not restricted to Great Britain. In 1986 the first Euro Bowl was held in Amsterdam, and clubs from the eight countries who make up the European Football League competed. As well as a British representative, there were teams from the

Netherlands, Switzerland, Finland, West Germany, Italy, Austria and France. The Finns were victorious and indeed the game is strong there – Finland's national team had previously beaten Italy in the Nations Cup, contested by European countries.

Britain may well be in the vanguard in Europe as far as interest in the professional game is concerned but, as yet, we do not have the experience of other European nations, who have picked up the game from American servicemen and have been playing it on an organized basis since the Second World War.

Unlike Britain, no other major European television network broadcasts weekly programmes, although the Super Bowl – either as a live transmission or as highlights – is screened in most countries in mainland Europe.

11 THE MEN IN CHARGE

IT IS some measure of how complicated the game of American football is that seven officials are needed to control a match. They comprise the referee, the umpire, the head linesman, the line judge, the field judge, the back judge and the side judge.

Each one has his own very specific role, with the referee the man in overall charge. Every member of this seven-man team – often called the 'Zebras' because of their black-and-white striped shirts – also has a set position and, with television replaying any controversial incident in slow motion and from every conceivable angle, the pressure is just as intense for them as it is for the players.

There are more than 100 officials in the NFL, some of whom have a full-time job as well. They receive about $300 (1986) for each game but can travel up to 100,000 miles during the course of a season. Considering that every official must be fully conversant with all 1,800 rules in the NFL rule-book, and apply them perfectly in a game in which the action is often frenzied and confused, it can be seen that the rewards are not great.

Very often they are condemned by the evidence of slow-motion television, but from the beginning of the 1986 season they put the video to their own use. An instant replay video-recorder acts almost like an eighth official, and if the referee is in doubt about a major incident, he can ask for clarification from an observer who is studying a slow motion video recording. This was meant to rule out the possibility of disputed penalties but regular breakdowns in communication between the referee and the video official only brought more controversy, and the move found much opposition within the NFL.

Such electronic gadgetry is in sharp contrast to the game's formative days, when only three men officiated. Down the years, officials have been added one at a time until, in 1977, the present number were brought in.

While each has a different task, they all carry in their back pocket a yellow handkerchief, which they throw to the ground when they spot a rule infringement.

Their respective jobs are as follows:

The *referee* is the head man. He signals all fouls and, by using a microphone, explains each decision to the crowd. He has the final say on any disputed decision and liaises with the video official via a telephone-link, should the occasion merit it. He takes up a position directly behind the quarterback, and about 10 yards back from the line of scrimmage. From here he can survey the whole pitch.

The *umpire* stands directly opposite the referee on the other side of the line of scrimmage, 5 yards behind the defensive linemen. His task is to place the ball on the spot for each down and then he looks out for false starts at the line of scrimmage (players moving before the ball is in play) and checks the legality of the blocking.

The *head linesman* also keeps a check on infringements at the line of scrimmage. He is in charge of the 'chain crew',

The Men in Charge

the men on the sidelines who have a chain which measures 10 yards and which is brought on the field to ascertain whether a team has achieved its first down. He stands towards the sidelines and watches for out of bounds and other infringements.

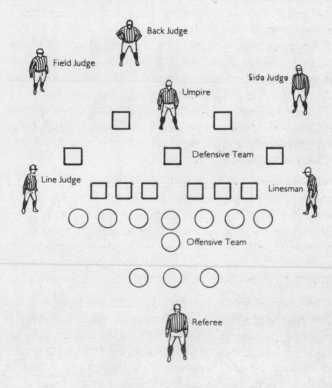

The *line judge* keeps his own stop-watch just in case the official game clock is faulty. He stands on the opposite side of the pitch from the head linesman and keeps a close

The Puffin Book of American Football

OFFICIAL SIGNALS

Touchdown, field goal, or successful try   First down (towards defensive team's goal)   Safety   Time out   Holding

Penalty refused, incomplete pass, play over, or missed goal (hands moved horizontally)   Illegal use of hands, arms or body   Intentional grounding of pass (parallel arms moved diagonally across body)   Personal foul (striking wrists together)   Interference with forward pass, or fair catch

Offside, or encroaching   Illegal motion at snap (hand moved in horizontal arc)   Illegal contact   Blocking below waist (preceded by personal-foul signal)   Ineligible receiver, or ineligible member of kicking team downfield

The Men in Charge

watch on the wide receivers and the men covering them to rule on out of bounds and other infringements in any play which comes towards his area of the pitch.

The *field judge* stands about 15 yards back from the line judge, on the defense side of the line of scrimmage, but out wide. He rules on plays which come near him.

The *back judge* also has a stop-watch, to enable him to time the 30-second interval between plays. He stands the furthest back on the defense side, up to 25 yards behind the line of scrimmage. He decides whether a field goal is successful or not and also keeps a watch on illegal blocking or holding. Together with the field judge, he also rules on pass interference, that is when a defensive player obstructs an attacking receiver to prevent him catching the ball.

The final member of the team is the *side judge*, and he was the last official brought into the game, in 1977. He stands on the same side as the head linesman, some distance further back, on the defensive side of the line of scrimmage. He shares a lot of the responsibility with the back judge for ruling on illegal blocking and focuses especially on punt returning.

12 TRAINING

IN ORDER to compete at the highest level of professional American football, a player must be at his physical peak. Even those who play in positions where the accent is on bulk and strength must have a level of performance that could put other athletes to shame.

Great emphasis is put on speed, stamina and strength, and before a coach even begins to contemplate which tactics he is going to adopt, his squad of players must be in supreme condition. Much of the work in bringing players up to the right pitch is undertaken long before the season starts.

For American professional players, the first step towards ultra-fitness is taken before summer camp, a pre-season training period which generally commences in July. In the weeks before the summer camp, players build up their general levels of fitness and stamina by road-running and weight-training. They also attempt to keep to their optimum weights which, for the various positions, are:

Running back – between 210 lbs and 235 lbs
Quarterback – can be any shape or size, but preferably 210–220 lbs
Wide receiver – around 200 lbs
Tight end – 240–250 lbs

Training

Centre – 265 lbs
Tackle – 275 lbs
Guard – 250 lbs
Linebacker – 220 lbs
Defensive tackle 270 lbs
Defensive end – 250 lbs
Safety – 200 lbs
Cornerback – 185 lbs
Kicker – can be any shape or size

Obviously, these are ideal, target weights and, in any position, a player may be some way from the optimum but, because of his height, may still have the perfect physique. Either way, each player is given his own target weight by his club's coaches and it is his job to turn up at summer camp as near as possible to that figure.

The players in specialized positions are also given a schedule of exercises custom-designed to sharpen up their particular skills. Each player runs an average of 2 miles every day, and they often run wearing weight jackets – jackets loaded with weights from 10 lbs to 50 lbs – to build up their stamina. Other forms of weight training (lifting, bench-pressing) strengthen arms and legs.

The rookie college players join the veterans to take part in summer camp and, from the total of 100 players when camp begins, the clubs have to pick the forty-five who will be their starting line-up when the season opens in September. This process begins at the end of the first week of camp, when the coaches will tell up to thirty of the original 100 that they have not got the necessary attributes to be part of the team. Further cuts are made in the second and third weeks, bringing the total down to around fifty-five, from which the final line-up will be chosen.

From the beginning of the fourth week to the announcement of the forty-five-man squad, the training becomes more intense, with more and more time spent on learning the various strategies and plays the team's coaches have devised. Clubs also have pre-season warm-up games against other NFL teams to try out some of the players who might be considered for a starting place.

The physical work is never slackened, but often new players find the mental strain of learning the multitude of plays and signals just as demanding. Some teams have more than 300 set plays and each one must be learned by heart by the players involved in a particular play. The classroom looms as large as the gymnasium in the build-up to the regular season.

A typical routine at summer camp would be that, after breakfast, the players would be split up into their respective units – offensive, defensive, special teams – and then spend most of the morning learning tactics and strategy. Training and work with the ball would take place either side of lunch, followed by an hour or so in the gymnasium before dinner. The players return to the classroom to continue their learning process before lights go out at 10 p.m. This regime, as punishing as the army, is designed to ensure that, come the start of the season, every squad member is fit, both physically and mentally.

The team of coaches – most clubs have a head coach and anything up to a dozen assistants covering all areas of the game – employ all sorts of technical aids in training and grading the players. Gymnasiums are equipped to the highest possible standards, video films are used to point out and correct faults and, perhaps most important, stopwatches are used to time players in every position.

For instance, as well as every team member being timed

Training

for speed over 40 yards, the quarterbacks are timed for how long it takes them to collect the ball from a snap and move back seven or so yards to pass the ball, receivers are timed over various short and long distances, and linemen are tested on weightlifting; how much they can lift and how long they can keep the weight above the head.

While summer camp represents possibly the most intensive training period in a footballer's year, the season itself is just as demanding. The morning after a match, the players are generally required to report to the club to watch video films of the action and to discuss what went wrong or right. Players nursing injuries are treated in the afternoon, while the others rest up.

From then on, the build-up begins towards the following weekend's game. There is no reduction in fitness and weight training but, as the game approaches, more and more time is spent in the classroom and on the training field, devising and practising the special plays that will be adopted to counter opponents' strong points and to exploit their weaknesses. To help this, the players watch extensive film of their opponents in action.

Diet is very important for a professional footballer, and most clubs employ a dietician who works out an eating regime for each player which helps them to keep to their target weight while building strength and stamina. Every week the players are all weighed and heavy fines are imposed on those who are above their target weight.

13 EQUIPMENT AND UNIFORM

AMERICAN FOOTBALL is one of the world's most physical and dangerous sports, and, in order to combat injuries, players must be properly kitted out and protected. The NFL – in an effort to cut down on the number of injuries sustained – lays down strict guidelines about player protection. To kit out a player is a very expensive business, and for an NFL club the bill for equipping the squad for a season can be up to $250,000.

Probably the most important part of a player's protection is the helmet, and that alone can cost more than $200. Most are tailor-made to a player's own specifications and are made from highly resistant moulded plastic. A faceguard is attached to the front and this can have a variety of designs, with bars to protect the nose and cheekbones in particular. It is made to fit absolutely tight to a player's head, and has an average life of about three seasons.

It was not until 1943 that the NFL insisted on the wearing of helmets, even though most players had already begun to use them. In the early days of the sport, heads went largely unprotected, with only a small number of players using leather caps, similar to rugby union scrum caps.

As the game has become more physical, so the need for greater protection has grown, and the modern helmet is

Equipment and Uniform

PROTECTIVE EQUIPMENT

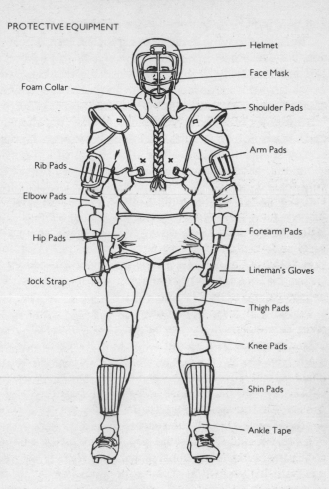

Helmet

Face Mask

Foam Collar

Shoulder Pads

Arm Pads

Rib Pads

Elbow Pads

Hip Pads

Forearm Pads

Jock Strap

Lineman's Gloves

Thigh Pads

Knee Pads

Shin Pads

Ankle Tape

designed to withstand the most violent collision. Inside every helmet is a layer of padding into which air is pumped and this acts like a shock absorber. Alternatively, glycol fluid can be injected, giving even more substantial cushioning.

The helmet may be the most conspicuous item of protection, but every player wears a huge amount of padding to safeguard his body. The biggest item is the shoulder pads, which give the modern American footballer the appearance of something between Mr Universe and The Incredible Hulk. Worn underneath the team jersey, the shoulder pads can weigh up to 6 lbs and are elaborate contraptions of plastic and foam; as well as offering protection for the shoulders they make players look even more huge than they actually are.

Collar pads, to protect the neck and collar bone, thigh pads, knee pads, hip pads, forearm pads, bicep pads and shin pads are all part of a team's armoury of safeguards for its players.

The quarterbacks, who are most often in the firing line, also sometimes wear a form of flak jacket, a padded jacket which protects their ribs, and knee braces, an elasticated, strengthened bandage which allows full movement of the joints and gives a good deal of protection.

Mouthguards, jockstraps – worn with a plastic protective box similar to that used by batsmen in cricket – and noseguards are part of most players' kit. Mouthguards are tailor-made for each team member, a wax impression having been taken of his mouth.

Added to the padding, players use a vast amount of tape to protect various parts of their body. Ankles are particularly suspect and so receive much taping. Up to 10 yards of tape can be used by one player on his ankles alone and it is estimated that, over the course of a season, a professional team uses more than 300 miles of tape. Wrists, knees and fingers are also well taped but players in different positions have different needs.

Equipment and Uniform

Offensive linemen tape their thumbs to their fingers in order to prevent them from illegally grabbing their opponents. Running backs and receivers usually do not tape their fingers, making it easier to catch the ball. Quarterbacks, who need to be as supple and free to move as possible, use very little tape, maybe just some to protect their ankles and wrists.

The high cost of kitting out a player is one of the problems faced by amateur teams competing in Britain. It can cost a player more than £300 for the basic equipment, before he starts to think about special items required for his particular position. It makes it all the more incredible that in 1987 there are around 6,000 fully kitted players in Britain.

14 FACTS AND TRIVIA

NAMES AND NICKNAMES

There has been no shortage of professional footballers whose names have been, shall we say, distinctive. Foremost among them is the great former San Francisco and New York Giants quarterback who rejoiced in the name of Yelberton Abraham Tittle. Not surprisingly, he was known as Y.A. Not far behind him in the name game were former players Elmer Bighead, Buzz Nutter and Vitamin T. Smith.

It seems that almost every well-known player has a nickname, but here are some of the more famous ones of past and present players: 'Broadway' Joe Namath (New York Jets 1965–76); O. J. 'The Juice' Simpson (Buffalo Bills 1969–77); Elroy 'Crazy Legs' Hirsch (Los Angeles Rams 1949–57); Earle 'Greasy' Neale (Philadelphia Eagles 1944–50). Still playing are: Walter 'Sweetness' Payton (Chicago Bears), William 'The Refrigerator' Perry (also Chicago), Ed 'Too Tall' Jones (Dallas Cowboys), Lawrence 'The Terminator' Taylor (New York Giants), Charles 'Too Mean' Martin (Green Bay Packers) and Billy 'White Shoes' Johnson (Atlanta Falcons).

As well as individual players receiving nicknames, various notorious units have been given collective names. The Chicago team of the early thirties were known as the

Facts and Trivia

'Monsters of the Midway'; the Minnesota defense of the early seventies were called 'The Purple People Eaters'; the formidable Pittsburgh defense of the seventies became known as 'The Steel Curtain'; the Denver defense of 1977 was 'The Orange Crush' and the New York Giants defense of 1986 was called 'The Big Blue Wrecking Crew'.

COLDEST GAME

For the 1901 play-off game at Cincinnati between the Bengals and the San Diego Chargers the temperature at River Front Stadium was recorded at $-9°C$ but, with a biting wind blowing, the wind-chill factor took the temperature down to $-39°C$. It was no surprise that the Chargers, who were used to sub-tropical temperatures, were unable to cope with the conditions and were beaten.

In 1948, the NFL championship game at Philadelphia was played in a fierce blizzard, the snow obscuring the lines and the referee having to use his judgement in the awarding of first downs. Play was possible only because the pitch had been covered with tarpaulin up until 30 minutes before kick-off. The players helped remove the tarpaulin.

LONGEST GAME

On Christmas Day, 1971, the play-off game between the Miami Dolphins and the Kansas City Chiefs was settled 22 minutes and 40 seconds into overtime. The total playing time was thus 82 minutes, 40 seconds, and the result was decided by a field goal which gave Miami a 27–24 victory.

BEST COMEBACK

In a regular season game in 1980, the San Francisco 49ers trailed the New Orleans Saints 35–7 at half-time. In the second half, the 49ers hit back to score 28 points without reply, tying the scores and taking the game into overtime before completing a remarkable comeback by winning the game with a field goal.

MOST ACCURATE KICKER

In eleven years with the San Francisco 49ers, Tommy Davis missed only two extra-point conversion kicks in 350 attempts, an incredible success rate of 99·43 per cent, by far the best record in NFL history. But Davis's career total of points pales by comparison with that of George Blanda who, in a 26-year career, kicked a total of 2,002 points for four different clubs, retiring in 1975 at the grand old age of 48.

LONGEST FIELD GOAL

Tom Dempsey, who was born with half his right foot missing, kicked the longest field goal in NFL history, an effort of 63 yards for New Orleans against Detroit in 1970. Dempsey's right boot, which he used for kicking, was specially made for him, and he clearly made light of his disability.

Facts and Trivia

LONGEST PASS PLAY

The longest possible pass play – i.e. the distance gained on a movement begun by a pass – is 99 yards, that being the distance from the team in possession's one-yard line and the opposition end zone. This has been achieved several times in NFL history, the last occasion being in 1985 when Philadelphia quarterback Ron Jaworski passed to set his side 99 yards upfield for a touchdown.

BIGGEST MISJUDGEMENT

The Houston Oilers cut a fourth-round draft choice called Steve Largent from their squad in 1977 because, timed over 40 yards, they felt he was too slow. Largent moved on to the Seattle Seahawks, where he has gone on to become one of the five leading wide receivers in the history of the game.

TALLEST AND SMALLEST PLAYERS

Dick Singh, at a shade over 7 feet, is thought to be the tallest man to have played regularly in the NFL. He was a tackle with the Cincinnati Bengals in the early 1980s. At the other end of the spectrum is 5-feet-tall Reggie Smith, a kicker with the Atlanta Falcons in the late seventies, who is probably the smallest man to have competed in the NFL.

FAMOUS EX-PLAYERS

Actor Burt Reynolds was an impressive running back for the Florida State University before deciding on a career in films. The renowned old-time singer and actor Paul Robeson was one of college football's most outstanding performers when at Rutgers between 1917 and 1918.

Famous politicians have also made their mark on the football field. President Ronald Reagan was a good college player at Eureka, Senator Edward Kennedy played for Harvard for two seasons and former President Gerald Ford was an outstanding member of the University of Michigan team of 1934 and was picked for the college all-star team.

GLOSSARY

BLITZ: A play called by the defensive side in an effort to prevent the quarterback from passing the ball. The blitz is also called the pass rush or 'dogging'.

BLOCKING: A defender is permitted to obstruct deliberately an attacking opponent who does not have the ball. This is blocking. However, it is illegal for a defender to grab or to hold an opposing player, or to trip him. Blocking must also be done head-on.

CLIPPING: An illegal block; when a defender tackles an attacker – other than the man with the ball – from the rear and below waist height.

COMPLETION: A pass thrown by the quarterback and safely caught by a player on his own side. If the ball hits the ground first or fails to go to hand, the pass is ruled incomplete.

DOWN: A down is the unit of play. Every time the ball-carrier is tackled to the ground or clearly cannot make further forward progress, play is stopped and restarted again with a set piece called a down or, more properly, a scrimmage. The two teams face each other at the mark where play was halted – the 'line of scrimmage' – and the game recommences with the attacking side setting the ball in motion. The team in possession is allowed four downs to make a minimum of 10 yards. See 'First down'.

ENCROACHING: When a defensive player at the line of scrimmage wrongly anticipates the resumption of play and lunges forward before the ball is in play, he is guilty of encroachment. His side is penalized by the loss of 5 yards.

END ZONE: The area at either end of the field where touchdowns are scored. A player must have possession of the ball in the end zone for a touchdown to be registered. The end zone is 30 feet deep.

FIELD GOAL: A field goal, worth three points, can be taken at any time by an attacking team in the course of an offensive drive. It normally occurs on the fourth down when the side in possession still has yardage to make up to claim a first down. A separate field-goal unit is brought on to the field, including a man to hold the ball for the kicker and players to protect the kicker from the onrushing defenders. A field goal can be attempted from any distance.

FIRST DOWN: When an attacking team gain 10 yards or more within their allotted four downs, they are given another four downs with which to continue their drive towards the opposition end zone. They are said to have achieved 'first down' and this process continues as the ball is driven upfield.

Glossary

FLAG: When an offence is adjudged to have been committed during a play, one of the game's seven officials throws a yellow handkerchief to the ground. This is known as 'a flag on the play'.

FUMBLE: An attacking player who loses the ball after having had it under control is said to have fumbled and the ball is up for grabs. It may be regained by the attacking side or a defender may gather it. If the latter is the case, it is called a 'turnover' and can often be a significant moment in a match.

HANG TIME: The period of time the ball spends in the air when it is punted. The longer the hang time, the more chance it gives the attacking players of following up the kick and putting the defending side's receiver under pressure.

HUDDLE: Before most plays, the attacking team group together, usually forming a circle, to take instructions on the forthcoming move. The huddle lasts no more than a few seconds. The defensive side may also go into a huddle to decide on their strategy.

IN MOTION: At the line of scrimmage, an attacking player may run laterally back and forth behind his side's front line in an attempt to confuse the defending side. He is said to be in motion. He may only move in a forward direction when the ball is in play.

INTENTIONAL GROUNDING: To avoid being tackled in possession and losing yardage (see 'sack') the quarterback sometimes throws the ball to ground. If it is not a genuine attempt to pass the ball (i.e. if it is not within five yards of an eligible receiver) the referee rules intentional grounding, an illegal play. The referee then offers the defending side two options; they can either ask the attacking side to recommence play from the mark where the ball was thrown to ground, or ask them to go back 10 yards from the spot where the illegal play began. Clearly, they choose whichever inflicts the biggest loss of yardage and, in either case, the attacking side also lose the down.

INTERCEPTION: The catching of an opponent's pass. The player who intercepts is allowed to run with the ball until he is tackled or scores a touchdown.

NEUTRAL ZONE: When the offensive and defensive lines come face to face at the line of scrimmage, there is a no-man's land which must not be entered until the ball is in play. The width of this neutral zone is the length of a football.

PERSONAL FOUL: This encompasses acts of violence outside the rules of the game – for instance, striking, kicking, or grabbing a face mask. Any unnecessary contact with an attacking player after he has been tackled, passed the ball or is out of bounds is also ruled a personal foul. In almost every case, a personal foul is punished by the loss of 15 yards for the defense and the award of a first down for the attacking side.

PUNT: When the team in possession is faced with losing the ball – on fourth down and still a number of yards short of achieving a first down – and when they are out of range of a field-goal attempt, they usually decide to punt the ball. A special team is brought on and the punter kicks the ball as high and as far as he can, transferring possession to the opposition but often deep in their own territory. See 'hang time'.

PUNT RETURN: The distance the ball is run back towards the punting team after it has been caught. Each side has its own special punt return team.

SACK: When the quarterback is caught in possession before he has had a chance to pass the ball, he is said to have been sacked. A sack inflicts a major loss of yardage on the side in possession. See 'blitz'.

SAFETY: When the side in possession have the ball deep in their territory, it is possible that one of their men could be tackled or held with the ball in his own end zone. If this occurs, a safety score – worth two points – is awarded to the defending side. On conceding a safety, the side with the ball must kick off from their 20-yard line.

SHOTGUN: In the usual formation at the line of scrimmage, the quarterback stands just behind the centre who commences the play by passing the ball back through his legs to the quarterback. In the shotgun formation, the quarterback stands several yards back from the line of scrimmage and the centre has to flick the ball to him. While this manoeuvre increases the risk of losing possession, it enables the quarterback to read the movements of the defensive side.

SNAP: The action of the centre transferring the ball through his legs to start the play.

SPECIAL TEAMS: Although only eleven players from each side are on the field of play at any time, each side has a squad of forty-five. They make up an attacking unit, a defensive unit and a special team. The special team are only brought on to the field for certain specific duties – restarts at the beginning of each half or after a score; punting; field goals; returning a punt; or an extra point kick after a touchdown.

TIME OUT: At the request of the captain of a side, a time out can be called and the game clock is stopped. This is either done to disrupt the rhythm of the opposition, to take instruction from the coaches, or simply for the attacking side to stop time ticking away towards the end of a game when the scores are close. Each side is allowed three time outs per half and they must last no longer than 1½ minutes.

TOUCHDOWN: A touchdown is awarded when a player from the attacking side either catches the ball in the end zone or runs with the ball into the end zone. It is worth six points. After scoring a touchdown, as in rugby, the successful side are allowed a conversion or 'extra point attempt' when they have to kick the ball between the posts. This is worth one point. Following a touchdown and extra point attempt, the side that just scored must kick off from the halfway line.

INDEX